When Two Se\ _

Andrew Watson

In memory of Dave Stubbings, a true Clash City Rocker

With thanks to Michelle for being here now and Ian for being there then

PROLOGUE

It was the best of years, it was the worst of years; it was my annus mirabilis, it was my annus horribilis; some of it inspired and excited me, some of it scared and saddened me.

Before that year, I was mostly scared all the time: scared of where I was growing up – I was not tough enough; scared of becoming an adult – school had started talking about careers; scared of life – my dad and sister were not the best examples.

Until that year, I had spent most of my time in my bedroom with David Bowie – not actually him, just his LPs; 1977 got me out of my bedroom, out of myself and out into the world; but by the end of the year, I was in disgrace.

I can remember that slow walk home from school in the middle of the day; slow so that they would have had time to phone my dad and tell him what had happened - so I did not have to. I suppose what happened was the logical conclusion of a year for which trouble had been prophesied because of the clash of the two sevens, a year that was not too promising from the start.

JANUARY

In the early hours of the first day of the year, I was laying prone on the floor. My head was hurting and my senses seemed to have failed me. The shape of a naval officer was slowly forming above me. It was like that scene at the end of the book we had been reading in English where the human prey is saved from the hunters by a man in a peaked cap, white cotton drill and gilt buttons. But this man was not asking if we had been having fun and games: he was shouting. I could not hear what he was shouting because my ears did not seem to be working properly; but I knew he was shouting because of his very red, angry face and the way his mouth was moving.

I managed to prop myself up onto my elbows and look around me. My man was not the only one dressed in white with a peaked cap: the dormitory was full of them. And all the teachers were there, too. And they were all shouting. As my ears began to function I could hear my RE teacher Mr Simmons' voice and the words, "disgrace... appalling behaviour... embarrassment... shameful."

I was not the only one being shouted at. I could see some of my schoolmates: a couple were, like me, on the floor; a few were in their bunks, limbs dangling; some were being held up by teachers, like casualties of war. When my sense of smell returned, there was the unmistakable stench of vomit mixed with something else, something that seemed unfamiliar. And then it came back to me: it was ouzo.

Ten hours earlier, we had been put ashore on the Greek island of Chios. Under a grey, out of season sky, the windswept waterfront was an unpromising place for a New Year's Eve shopping trip: a handful of tavernas were open and a solitary souvenir shop. But with the next scheduled stop a day away, a decision must have been made to prevent hundreds of teenagers going down with cabin fever. All day, the ship's tender had been ferrying groups to and from the cruise ship anchored outside the harbour; in the late afternoon it was the turn of our school. I am not sure who first tried to buy a bottle of ouzo from the old crone in the gift shop but, when he was successful, the realisation that we could get booze swept through the rest of our

1

group of fourteen and fifteen-year-old boys like a biblical plague. I did not know what ouzo was - the only alcohol I had drunk was Dad's horrible home brew – but when everyone queued up to buy a bottle, I did too.

I had not wanted to be on an RE school trip to the Holy Land, especially at Christmas, but my dad had been unusually keen to shell out the exorbitant amount of £120 to send me away on an educational cruise ship for two weeks. Heaven knows where he got the money from, although he had made me stump up for my spending money. Visiting Israel, Lebanon, Turkey and Greece would be the making of me, he said. He had travelled the world during his National Service and it had broadened his mind, he said. This was ironic as he was the most narrow-minded old bastard I knew.

The real reason I did not want to go was that no one I knew was going. The boys on the trip were all in the upper stream and from the middle class Victorian houses near the school – there was not even anyone from my estate that I vaguely knew. I had felt the odd one out from the moment we set off on the coach from school and had been homesick ever since. But what I found out for the first time, as we celebrated the New Year, was how easy it is to make friends when alcohol is involved; not only with the boys from my school who I had little in common with, but with kids from other schools.

I could not remember much after that but evidently word had spread around the New Year's Eve disco that the boys from a south-east London comprehensive were drinking more than Coca Cola. This made us lots of friends and, very quickly, the atmosphere turned to one of abandon as the potency of the ouzo made for some wild moves on the dance floor. It was the deputy Headmistress of a private girls' school in Kent who first noticed that something was wrong; some of her charges seemed to be in a near hysterical state and she had alerted the captain and crew that alcohol had been smuggled on board.

Sensing trouble, we had sought refuge in our dormitory deep in the hull of the ship hoping the storm would pass. The mistake we had made, once there, was to carry on going at the ouzo as if our lives depended on it. The captain and his senior officers had been moving from dorm to dorm to find the culprits behind the widespread

2

teenage drunkenness up above. When they arrived in our cabin, their search had ended. An entire dormitory of near catatonic boys greeted them; it must have looked like a scene from a Limehouse opium den.

The next morning, as I walked to breakfast, a girl I had never seen before fell in step alongside me and put her arm through mine. "Hi, Billy!" she said. She had big brown eyes, long dark hair and an impish face.

"Hi," I offered, tentatively.

"You're funny," she laughed.

"I don't feel too funny at the moment."

"Well, you were last night."

Not having a clue what her name was, but not wanting to reveal my ignorance – or my ouzo-induced lack of short term memory – I bluffed my way through the rest of the conversation. We seemed to be carrying on a dialogue that had started without me. She knew my dad worked in a biscuit factory; her father was in Wellington boots, which I thought was an odd thing to tell me until it became clear that her father owned a factory that manufactured them. We had a sort of connection, she said.

"Sophie!" a voice from behind us barked. The girl's face froze and she double-backed away from me, trotting after a ferocious looking woman in a tweed suit. Sophie. A girl. What had she meant by 'funny?' Funny peculiar? Or funny ha ha? She had linked arms with me; that must have meant ha ha not peculiar. And she had sought me out. And she looked pleased to see me. And she was pretty. This was good. Sophie. A girl. But how much more had I told her about myself? I hoped I had not said anything about my sister. Or my mum.

When I sat down with my continental breakfast, I asked the others if they could remember me talking to a girl. This immediately prompted some to recall girls from the private school they had spoken to and got telephone numbers from; others could only remember odd snatches of their own drunken behaviour; but none of them knew anything about me and Sophie. Worse news was that we were about to arrive in Crete and would spend the day looking at old ruins; in the evening, we were banned from the recreation area

3

because of our misdemeanours and would be confined to our dormitory; the next day we would be arriving in Athens and then flying home. There was every chance I would never see Sophie again; cruelly cut down before we had a chance to blossom.

I saw neither hide nor hair of Sophie that day. Sightseeing on Crete, I saw other school parties from the ship and searched their number for her face - but nothing. I wanted to confide in someone but the other boys in my group were not really my friends, despite our alcoholic camaraderie. I wanted to find out if Sophie was definitely one of the private school girls. I wanted to see her again just once before the trip ended. There was no sign of her in the mess at dinner and then, for the rest of the evening, we skulked in our dormitory, our teachers making sure we felt the mark of shame our booze smuggling and drunkenness deserved.

The day of departure dawned an iron grey and we were already docked at Piraeus. The ship thronged with activity: harassed teachers, schoolkids laden down with bags and cases, crew members scurrying about preparing for us to go ashore. It had been exactly 24 hours since I had – to my mind - first met Sophie and, in truth, I had sort of forgotten what she looked like; whenever I tried to conjure up her face in my mind, all I saw was Cherry from Pan's People.

We had to assemble on the upper decks in our school groups ready to disembark. I was late getting on deck but not many schools seemed to have made it on time either. As I walked past the other parties to where my school was assembled, I looked out for Sophie and the ferocious tweedy lady but I saw neither. I knew that my sense of heartbreak was ridiculous but that was how I felt. It was cold and it was raining and I felt like an actor in a cheap romance. But there was still the hope that I might see Sophie at the airport.

When I found my school, we immediately started to make our way to the gangplank. I asked Mr Simmons where the other schools were. "They're staying aboard," he said. "The ship is going on to Malta and they're flying home from there." So that was it. There was no chance: I would never see Sophie again.

When I got to the quayside I dumped my suitcase in the luggage hold at the back of the coach and trudged to the front to get on board.

4

As I looked up at the ship, I could hear my name being called. "Billy!" It was a girl's voice. The guardrails on the upper decks were packed with people. I scoured their faces. "Billy!" And there she was, smiling and waving. At me. Sophie. I frantically waved back and then Simmons bundled me on to the coach and we pulled away.

"You're such a wanker." Kev, supposedly my best friend, had listened to me pour my heart out about the tragedy of Sophie and the relationship that never was. It was great to be home.

"But we had a connection; she said so," I whined, realising that I sounded pathetic as I outlined my manufacturing link to Sophie.

"Your dad working in a biscuit factory is hardly the same as owning a factory that makes rubber goods," Kev observed as he trampled all over my feelings. "You're back here, now."

He was right. In the cold light of a south-east London winter's day, 24 hours after landing at Heathrow airport, the cruise and the fleeting encounter with Sophie seemed an irrelevance. There were more pressing concerns: school started again soon and I would have to take part in an assembly on the trip; it was less than two weeks until the new Bowie album was released and I was short of money; and the words my dad had greeted me with when he met the coach at school had really depressed me.

"Your sister's coming home," Dad had sighed, walking alongside me as I struggled with my suitcase all the way to our flat. Dad shrugged in reply when I asked him for how long. She had been evicted again but now she had her name on the waiting list and was hoping for an offer of a council flat soon. Deborah coming home again was terrible news. I had lost count of how many times she had moved in and out of our flat since she had first left, aged sixteen, five years before. Then, she had met Maurice – or Mole, as the tosser liked to call himself – and had disappeared into a life of squatting for six months. Acting on information from her friends, me and Mum had been on countless bus journeys trying to track her down – Peckham, Camberwell, South Norwood, Brixton – but she always seemed to have just left and the search would be abandoned until a fresh sighting was reported.

5

Then she had turned up on our doorstep with two startling changes to her appearance: a bright orange Ziggy Stardust haircut and a distended belly. I could not help being impressed by the first, and I always credited that moment as being the start of my fascination with Bowie; but I found her pregnancy mortifying. A ten-year-old boy's sense of morality is fairly rudimentary but I knew that this was bad, not in itself, but bad for Deborah as the wagging tongues on the estate would be harsh in their judgement of her and of us, her family. I could tell Dad was furious, and he would have probably turned her away if it was not for Mum.

No one ever said that Deborah's behaviour killed Mum, but I had thought it on more than one occasion. To die of heart disease at the age of forty seemed a bit of a coincidence when it was obvious her daughter had broken her heart. When the baby was born Mum had doted on him but there had been a sadness about her from the moment Deborah had moved back home and she had never recovered from the stroke she had on little Michael's first birthday.

Deborah had moved out soon after when she was reconciled with Mole but the last four years had been a succession of grotty flats, rent arrears, evictions and returns home. Dad just about tolerated her homecoming every time – but I hated it: sometimes Mole moved in as well and I always ended up looking after Michael in the evenings when Deborah went to work in the pub and Dad and Mole went to drink in it.

"You didn't miss much at the football – two draws – although there was a good scrap with the away fans on New Year's Day but, more importantly, listen to this," Kev said with a grin on his face. "This will take your mind off girls from posh schools."

Kev took a single from his pile on the windowsill. It had a plain black sleeve with no hole for the label to show through. When he pulled the disc out, I saw the beige and red logo of EMI, which disappointed me as I immediately associated it with the awful Queen. It made me want to go home and get my Bowie LPs out of their sleeves and look at the warm, comforting orange of the RCA label. When he put it on, the arm of his record player bounced around as the click and crackle coming from the speakers told me that Kev had them turned up loud. And then: a crash of deafening guitar, a roll of thundering drums and a threatening voice intoning, "Right, now!" followed by a demonic cackle. What was this? And then the singer – singer? – started saying he was an anti-Christ and an anarchist – what was an anarchist? – and that he wanted to destroy passers-by and then he said he wanted to stop the traffic and he kept saying he wanted to be anarchy and that anarchy was coming sometime for the UK and then he listed things I had heard on the news, like MPLA, UDA, IRA, and then he mentioned the NME and then he said he wanted to get pissed and then it all came to a shuddering and chaotic end.

All the while Kev had been staring intently at my face with a stupid silent laugh on his. "What do you think? The singer's called Johnny Rotten. It's fucking brilliant, isn't it"?

"It's…"

"They're called the Sex Pistols. The punk rock group that swore on the local news before Christmas. You didn't see it but your dad did and he said, in his usual logical way, they should be shot and put in the army."

"It's…"

"By the way, did you know your dad went away to Brighton for Christmas with Tina Breakspear's mum?"

I felt like I had been punched in the face, not once but twice, and with a great big red cartoon boxing glove with a horseshoe hidden inside. I struggled to know which blow to deal with first. So that was why my dad had forked out for me to go on the school trip: he wanted me out of the way so he could have a dirty time at the seaside. Why did it have to be Tina's mum? Tina lived on the landing below us with her dad; her mum had left a couple of years ago soon after she started wearing bright red lipstick all the time. I would never be able to look Tina in the eye again. I wished my dad had told me himself but I did not care what he had done. He led a miserable existence and was entitled to have a little excitement.

Excitement. That was the feeling that Kev's record had given me. I had never heard anything like it. It was insane. I did not know people were allowed to make music like that. It was out of control. The singer was like one of those blokes ranting at Speakers' Corner and he sounded like he came from London. And the stuff he was going on about: getting what you want, shopping schemes, council tenancies. It was out of this world but it was very much of this world; it made no sense but it made complete sense; it was wonderful.

School: tatty, stuffy and stifling. It started again with an assembly for the 4th Year from the Headmaster, old Burkett. He droned on and on about O levels next year and the decisions we had to start making now. Were we thinking about a career in manufacturing or engineering? Or did we have a clerical and administrative path in mind? I had nothing in my mind except Sophie, the new Bowie album and, now, the Sex Pistols. I had no clue what job I wanted when I left school. In truth, I did not want a job at all. What I had seen of the jobs Dad and Deborah had, they seemed pretty bloody dull, to me. Long, repetitive hours for just enough reward to keep the wolf from the door, as Dad often said.

"Monson!" It was Simmons. "Break time in my classroom. We're having a meeting about the assembly on the Holy Land trip. Don't forget and don't be late."

I told him that I would be there and I wrote it on the back of my hand to show some commitment; but the prospect filled me with dread. Getting up on the stage with all those middle-class kids, in front of the whole school, and waffling on about the miracle of being in Bethlehem on Christmas Day; I would be a laughing stock.

I got off fairly lightly. I came away from the meeting with just one phrase to learn: "From the port of Haifa we headed inland to follow in the footsteps of Jesus." Embarrassing but brief. If I could stand still and keep my head down while I delivered my line, my part could be over before anyone spotted it was me. I could not worry about it too much, though: Simmons had to have his slide show developed first so it was a few weeks away.

After school on the second Monday back, I walked to the High Street instead of going straight home. It had been a year since I had visited the record shop and that was when I went to buy the last Bowie LP. That had only six tracks on it so I was hoping for a little more from the new album. Deborah and Mole had moved back into our flat and I had looked after Michael several times so Mole had given me some money.

I loved and hated going to the record shop: loved it because it was where I had bought my first T Rex singles before Deborah had told me Marc Bolan was a waste of time and that it was David Bowie I should be listening to. I had saved up to buy *The Rise and Fall of Ziggy Stardust and the Spiders from Mars* and, from then on, I had become an album-buyer. But the man in the shop was always so unfriendly that what should have been a joyous experience was always an intimidating one for me.

The LP was in the window. It was called *Low*. The cover was orange and had a shot of Bowie in profile wearing, what looked like, a duffle coat and with a floppy haircut. It was from the film he had been in when he played an alien; I had not seen it because it had an X certificate.

In the shop, I found the cover in the rack and took it to the grumpy bloke behind the counter. He silently took a copy down from the shelf behind him, put it in a bag for me and I paid my £2.49. Realising I still had enough money for a single, I asked him if he had Anarchy in the UK by the Sex Pistols. I thought it was not possible for his miserable face to fall any further, but somehow it did.

"No," he growled. "Not in this shop. Not that punk rock rubbish. Bloody awful. They can't play a note. And anyway, you can't get that, now. It's been deleted. And so have they. By their record company." I backed away out of the shop leaving him muttering to himself.

Outside, I took the LP out and threw the bag away. I tucked it under my arm as I walked down the High Street because I wanted as many people as possible to see that I had the new David Bowie record. A few looked at it but none of them showed any signs of being impressed. They probably were but were just trying to hide it out of envy.

I went straight round to Kev's so we could listen to *Low* together. The first and last tracks on side one had no singing on them but the five in between were great. They were all quite short and quirky. The music was different from his last LP - more loose sounding - and there were some strange sound effects; but the drumming was incredible and the lyrics were peculiar – more so than normal: on one song Bowie was singing about drawing awful things on the carpet and on another he sang about his blue room, which I liked because my bedroom was blue. There was a song about crashing his car and another asking someone to be his wife.

Side two was something of a shock: there was hardly any singing on the four long tracks, except for a bit of warbling on the first and last ones. It was very electronic and sounded like classical music. Kev kept pulling faces and it was obvious what he thought.

To avoid hearing anything critical when the LP had finished, I changed the subject and told Kev that I had tried to buy the Sex Pistols' single but could not understand why the record shop owner had reacted as he did. He said his brother had bought it for him from a stall at Petticoat Lane and that we should go there because they also sold punk clothes. I had not been to Petticoat Lane market since Mum died; I used to go there a lot with her when I was little – I used to love the hustle and bustle. I said to Kev I was not too sure what punk clothes were like but, if the music was anything to go by, there was a good chance they would be unsettling. As I was leaving, Kev said there was a programme on the telly at Sunday lunchtime about punk and that I should watch it – then I would understand.

When the programme was on I had the flat to myself: Dad was at the pub and the others had gone out somewhere in Mole's old van. It started off talking about punk rock and then showed some film of the Sex Pistols playing a concert; the lead singer's behaviour was as demented as he had sounded and he looked ugly and beautiful at the same time. He had orange hair like Bowie used to have but his clothes were scruffy and aggressive. The audience were dressed in a strange way, too, and a lot of them had dyed and spiky hair. They were not so much dancing to the music as having a bundle. How did I not know about these people? The reporter said youngsters were attracted to punk rock because groups like Led Zeppelin were remote from their fans. I wondered what Kev was thinking because he liked bands like that. Then she interviewed the Sex Pistols and they seemed to not be paying much attention. They spoke in the same way that I did and they were shy but confident at the same time. The reporter interviewed another group called The Clash. They spoke like me, as well. She asked them what they wrote songs about and they said, what's going on at the moment. The reporter said one of their songs had the line, "Everybody does what they're told to," and asked them if they thought young people had been pushed around. When the youngest-looking one in the band answered he said that the school he went to was no good and the kids learnt nothing; all they were working for was to go to a factory around the corner. He said most of his mates were working in factories and he looked angry and sad as he said it. When he had finished speaking, I could not concentrate on the rest of the programme because a light had come on somewhere in my head; not a light, more an illuminated sign. What the sign said was unclear - the letters were blurred - but, nevertheless, it was there and it was shining brightly.

FEBRUARY

If I thought that the pain of meeting and being parted from Sophie all within 36 hours would be eased by a new David Bowie LP and the excitement of punk rock, I was wrong. It was true that both of these things were in my thoughts but I was preoccupied with Sophie and whenever I thought of her, I still smarted. I never really had the opportunity to speak to girls: I went to a boys' school, I never went to the youth club and I was intimidated by the confident and assured girls on the estate. Mostly, I went unnoticed; my clothes and hair were average and I was not hard, a quality which, for some reason, impressed girls. It all felt so cruel: I had no recollection of my first conversation with Sophie and our second had been cut short. I ran through what had been said countless times. I was holding on to it like a souvenir - a souvenir of something that had been and gone forever. At heart, I knew it was hopeless - I should just forget about her; but it was impossible. I was finding it harder than usual to concentrate in class and when I went to bed I could not sleep; the feeling of loss and longing gnawed away at me in the dark. On more than one occasion, I woke up thinking it must be nearly morning only to see that it had just turned midnight. I would switch on my light and read. I was reading *Nineteen Eighty-Four* by George Orwell because Mole had told me that some of the songs on Bowie's *Diamond Dogs* LP were about the book. It was hard going, and some of it I struggled to understand, but I sort of identified with Winston Smith. He was isolated and was the only person who thought in the way he did but then he found Julia. I started to think of me and Sophie as Winston and Julia and sometimes I played one of the Bowie songs about them; it was a really sad one called Rock 'n' Roll With Me and it just made me feel even more miserable. Dad kept coming home from the pub late so even he had noticed that I was getting up in the night and how tired I was in the morning; it was making me ill.

I hated the big assembly on Monday mornings: I was half asleep and I could never pay attention to what was being said at the best of times. The Holy Land trip assembly was an even worse prospect because, even though I would be up on the stage with Simmons and the others, I knew I would still struggle to follow what was going on. The whole thing made me feel slightly sick.

I went straight to the hall rather than go to my form room because I had to help with the preparation. Simmons was up on the stage fiddling about with a slide projector and looking at some notes. He was going to be giving the bulk of the assembly, explaining about each place we visited and its biblical or ancient historical significance. Us pupils had the simple task of making short narrating links. I only had one, most of the others had two or three.

My cue was Colin Cummings saying, "The eastern Mediterranean was calm as we sailed towards the coast of Israel." Cummings was one of those sporty kids who tried to pretend he was a hippy. He walked around with an army haversack on his shoulder, with the names of bands like Yes and Genesis written on it, and he smelled faintly of patchouli oil. I had to stand next to him; the smell made me feel more nauseous than ever. Everyone started filing into the hall and I could see Kev grinning in my direction with anticipation. I knew what he was thinking: look at him up on the stage, standing next to that tosser, Colin Cummings.

I was bored within minutes of the presentation starting. Simmons was droning on about the flight to Italy and then the Oracle at Delphi. The projector was making a soporific whirring noise and a loud clunk every time it changed slides. I could see specks of dusk dancing around in the beam of light. I felt ill and tired.

I was snapped out of my reverie by Cummings puffing up his chest and bracing himself to deliver his line. As he finished, the projector clunked and I glanced up at the picture on the screen. It was a photograph Simmons had taken of us on the harbourside at Haifa waiting to get on a coach. I could see myself standing slightly apart from the group on the left of the picture. What I could also see on the right of the picture was the edge of the school group getting on the coach behind ours. It was a party of girls and two of them were holding each other in mid-laugh and looking towards the camera. One of them had long dark hair. It was Sophie. Sophie.

When Cummings jabbed me in the ribs with his elbow, I realised I had said her name out loud. Twice. I heard a ripple of laughter run across the hall and Simmons say my name. I looked across at him. "From the port of Haifa…" he hissed between gritted teeth.

"From the port of Haifa we headed inland to follow in the footsteps of Jesus," I loudly proclaimed. The ripple of laughter became a torrent. I walked to the side of the stage and threw up in Colin Cummings' haversack.

"What's wrong with you, man? You look like you've lost a pound and found a penny." Mole was in the front room when I got home from school, hunched over the electric fire like an old man, smoking a fag. I loathed the way he smoked: he cupped the cigarette in his hand so the tip was almost touching his palm. There were a lot of things I disliked about Mole – the fact he called me "man" for one - but mostly I hated that his David Bowie look had mutated into Catweazle; he looked dreadful.

Deborah had first met him in a pub one night after work. She had only just turned sixteen and had been working at an office in the City for two weeks. Mole was working on one of the building sites. The day after she met him, she never came home from work. Mum and Dad were beside themselves and reported her missing to the police. The police asked them to check her belongings and they realised she had taken some clothes, make-up and, crucially, her toothbrush. They expected her to come home the next day after work but they found out she had not gone to work. She never went back to her office job and we saw nothing of her; for six months we only heard about her until she reappeared with orange hair and a baby on the way; I felt both awestruck and appalled. She had told me that Mole had a David Bowie haircut when she met him and she had fallen in love with him instantly. Deborah said he was fun and did not worry about anything; he was living in a squat in Brixton and only worked when he needed to. She went off with him because it was a much more exciting way of living than being an office girl waiting to get married and have kids; but getting pregnant had quickly brought her exciting way of life to an end and, from what I saw, she had not had much fun since.

If Mole had been carefree when Deborah met him, I had never seen that side of him; he seemed on edge to me, especially when he was out of work, which he often was. I found him childish: he was always talking in stupid voices after he had been to the pub and, in the times they lived with us, I sometimes heard him crying in their bedroom when they had rows. He was 21 when he met Deborah. I found it creepy that a man of his age would be interested in a 16-year-old but my sister said there was nothing wrong with it; she was very protective of him, even though they had kept splitting up and getting back together again. She said he came from a broken home but never said in what way it was broken or who had broken it. I sometimes felt like he had broken mine but that was probably unfair. Mole tried hard to be like an older brother: talking to me about music and football. He kept suggesting groups I should listen to but it was all hard rock and I never took him up on his offers to borrow LPs. He once came to football with me and Dad but he had no idea and was a bit of an embarrassment, getting players' names wrong and shouting out at inappropriate moments.

"Is it because your team lost on Saturday?" he tried again when I did not answer. He always made a comment about the football; because I went he thought I was interested in it - but I was not. Dad first took me when I was 7 and, although I went to matches with Kev now, I went out of loyalty to my dad so we would have something in common to talk about. I also went because everyone on the estate did and if I stopped going I would fit in even less. I enjoyed the atmosphere and the sense of togetherness: when it rained and everyone crowded under cover at the back of the terraces, the singing gave me goose pimples; but I found the actual football boring.

I ignored Mole and went to my room. I laid on my bed and thought about the events of the day as I traced the cracks in the ceiling. The assembly had been a disaster and afterwards I had been dogged between lessons by boys sniggering after me in the corridors or, more embarrassingly, shouting out. Mostly, it was "Sophie!" but it was also "Jesus freak!" or just plain "wanker!" When I saw Kev, he had simply put his arm around my shoulder, sighed and shook his head. If he was intending to make me feel better, his silence only made me feel worse. To keep out of everyone's way, I stayed in one of the art rooms at lunchtime under the pretence that I was catching up on some work; but I could tell in the afternoon lessons that it was all around the school that I had a crush on some girl that I had barely spoken to.

I put on *Aladdin Sane* and read some of *Nineteen Eighty-Four* but then the song Drive-In Saturday came on and I started to imagine it was about me and Sophie and I lost my concentration. I just lay there feeling sorry for myself until the door opened and Deborah stuck her head into the room. "What do you want for your birthday?" she said with a complete lack of enthusiasm. My birthday. In a week's time. Well, it was certain that I would reach 15 never having been out with a girl. What a prat. It struck me that I had no idea how old Sophie was. She had looked about my age but girls had a habit of looking older than they were. She could be 13; that would be embarrassing. And then I realised it was not important: I was not going to see Sophie ever again. "And by the way," Deborah added, "we've been offered a flat by the council."

For once, there was a tepid glow of expectation in my life. My sister, Mole and little Michael were moving to the next estate, which meant that me and Dad would have our flat to ourselves again; more importantly, as this time they had got a council flat, they were less likely to get evicted and come back to live with us. The downside of this was Deborah's intention to have a big housewarming party. She was expecting me to go even though there would be no one there of my age. However, there were other positives: my birthday would ensure I got some money and it was going to coincide with my trip to Petticoat Lane with Kev. His brother had assured him that there were a couple of stalls that sold punk stuff and I was going to buy some singles because there were no punk LPs. Kev said albums were too long and boring, which struck me as strange for someone who listened to hard rock where everything was long and boring. I thought I might buy some clothes because, since I had watched the television documentary, I had noticed a couple of people who looked like they might be punks: there was a bloke I passed waiting at the

16

bus stop some mornings who wore narrow jeans and had short spiky hair; and there was a girl who worked in the hairdressers on the High Street who had very dark eye make-up and very short, very blonde hair. She wore tight black trousers and, like the bloke at the bus stop, they were not flares. I wore flares; everyone I knew wore flares. These two looked so different, just because of their trousers. I wanted a pair of trousers that were not flares.

It was so cold waiting at the bus stop with Kev and his brother that I kept getting violent shudders and intermittently my teeth would chatter. Gary kept laughing and pointing at me each time it happened and told me I should have worn a proper coat. He sounded like my dad but he had a point: I was wearing a stupid little bomber jacket with a t-shirt underneath. He was wearing his sheepskin and even Kev was buried in a cagoule. It was early on a Sunday morning and we were waiting in the deserted High Street for a 47 bus. Everywhere, there were signs of the previous day's market for the eyes and nose to savour: piles of half-empty fruit and veg boxes stood like sentries at the pavement's edge and the stench of rotting cabbage and decaying bananas filled the air. We were heading to Petticoat Lane, a much bigger but less smelly street market of clothes stalls, north of the river. I had my birthday money and I wanted to buy the Sex Pistols record and a pair of trousers.

I used to go to Petticoat Lane with Mum and it was always a shock to arrive: the bus having trundled up through the deserted Sunday morning streets of south London and the City, to suddenly come across so many people, all squashed into two roads, was like being an explorer and unexpectedly finding a forgotten tribe. Gary said he would show us the stall where he bought the Sex Pistols record and then he would see us later as he had a few things to do. We passed a pub down a side street and he said we should meet him outside there at midday.

When we got to the record stall, I was disappointed: I was not sure what I was expecting but it was not a miserable-looking bloke, a bit like the one in my local record shop, selling Rod Stewart and Elton John LPs. But there was a cardboard box at the side of the stall with PUNK & GARAGE ROCK written on it with a handful of LPs and singles inside. The singles all had sleeves with pictures on like they were mini-LPs. I looked through them but there were no Sex Pistols ones. The stallholder turned out to be quite helpful: he said Anarchy In The UK was hard to get now and most of the punk records he had were American. He pulled out two LPs but neither group looked like the punks I had seen on the telly. The first one was by New York Dolls and they were dressed Glam and had long hair; the second was by Ramones and they were wearing leather jackets and jeans. What really caught my eye was that their jeans were not flares – they were tight at the ankles and ripped at the knees. They looked so tough, I bought the LP even though I had never heard them. I kept it in the carrier bag because it was bright orange with 'Roy's Records' written on it; it looked pretty good.

"You'll like them," Kev said. "I heard them on John Peel this week." He bought two singles: one by The Damned, who all had paper bags on their heads on the cover, and the other by Buzzcocks, who looked quite normal.

"I suppose you heard those on John Peel, too. What is John Peel?" I asked him as we walked away from the stall.

"Not what, who. Late night, Radio 1? You need to get out of your Bowie bubble and open your ears," he sneered.

"How long have you been listening to it, then?" I snapped back.

"Since Monday," he said shamefaced.

But Kev was right; I had been living in a bubble: I went to school, went to football and the rest of the time I spent in my room reading or listening to my Bowie records. Kev tried to get me to listen to other groups, go to the youth club, the pictures, anything; but I wasn't interested. It had been like that for the last few years and I had not done much else. Dad took me to the theatre at the Town Hall, once, to see Morecombe and Wise; but that was about the only digression from routine that I could recall, apart from the Holy Land trip. They had been hilarious, particularly Eric: he came on stage throwing small objects up in the air and catching them in a brown paper bag. Only there were no objects; he was throwing nothing and flicking the bag with his thumb and finger to make it look like an impact. It went on and on and the pretend objects were thrown higher and higher and they took ages to come down but still he caught them and all the while he said nothing. I laughed so much I struggled for breath and Dad was laughing too; he kept throwing his head back and snorting. It was the funniest thing we had ever seen.

Someone bashed into me in the crush and I dropped my LP. There were so many people, I thought it would get trampled on but Kev was down quickly and retrieved it for me. "Wake up, Billy. You're like a tit in a trance," he chided. "We need to find this clothes stall."

There were so many stalls, though, and all the traders were shouting about their goods and competing with each other to be heard. It was a bit overwhelming and made my head spin. I was on the verge of telling Kev we should go home when he nudged me, pointed and said, "Let's follow him."

'Him' was a boy, probably two or three years older than me, with spiky hair that seemed to be dyed two different colours: blonde and an orangey brown. I could not see what he was wearing but his head looked pretty punky; we could only see the back of it as he moved at speed through the crowds and I noticed that people coming the other way kept giving him funny looks as he passed them.

Eventually, he stopped at a stall and I could see he was wearing an old suit jacket, a t-shirt underneath that looked like he had painted it himself and narrow jeans. The stall was run by a man who looked like a biker. He was wearing a leather jacket like the ones on the cover of my new LP and had greasy quiffed hair and thick-soled Teddy Boy shoes. There were lots of leather jackets on his stall and pairs of straight-legged trousers. We were in the right place.

Kev bought a pair of denim jeans and I bought some trousers that were like jeans but they were black and had a loop on one leg and a long, narrow pocket on the other. "They're for your hammer and your chisel," the stallholder laughed, but I was not sure what he meant so I just smiled at him and nodded. What I was sure of was that we had trousers that were not flares; we were different now.

We were too early to meet Gary so we wandered around the market looking at the stalls. A lot of the stallholders called out to passing people to come and look at their goods and others had big crowds around them. One man was selling sheets and pillowcases and he was making a big show of how cheap they were. He piled up a big bundle of them and was shouting, "Who'll give me a quid for the lot?" Nobody answered but he kept on shouting; then a man at the back of the crowd called out, "I will!" and held out a pound note. As soon as he did, loads of other people started waving pound notes and a boy helping the stallholder went around the crowd taking the money as the man threw the bundles to each of the buyers. At another stall, a man was selling plates and bowls and cups in the same way. He built a tower out of them and it wavered and wobbled around and looked as though it would fall. The crowd oohed and aahed every time it was about to topple over; but it never did – it was like a show.

We waited outside the pub for Gary. It seemed to be getting even colder and he eventually turned up half an hour late. He had a girl with him. A punk girl. And she was not dressed for the weather. "This is Mags," he said, indicating the girl with his thumb. He turned to her, smiling. "These two fancy themselves as punks."

"Oh, yeah?" Mags did not seem impressed.

"Yeah," Gary laughed. "What did you buy?" We showed him the records and trousers. He pointed at my Ramones LP and said, "That is a blinding record. Gets me right in the mood, it does."

He did not say in the mood for what but, knowing Gary, he probably meant drinking or fighting.

Mags held up my trousers. "These are alright," she nodded, "but you should put some zips in them. And you need to get rid of that centre parting. And get some monkey boots. Or plastic sandals. And you…" she said looking at Kev.

"Come on," Gary interrupted, "let's have a couple of pints." We were going in the pub? Me and Kev would never get served. This did not look too promising: my experience with booze was pretty limited and the last time was the New Year's Eve ouzo fiasco. Also, I had never been in a pub, only outside one with a bottle of Coke while Dad was inside drinking gallons of beer with his mates before football.

Gary pushed open the door and we followed him in. It was incredibly dark inside and had a sickly, stale smell of beer and cigarettes. As my eyes adjusted to the smoky light, I could see that the pub was very old-fashioned: there was a lot of dark wood with etched glass panels dividing the tables where people sat; it was lit by dim yellow globes that reflected in the mirrors on the wall behind the bar. What comforted me was that it was quite crowded – mostly with old men but it was busy. Coupled with the gloominess, it made me feel less apprehensive: we were inconspicuous.

Gary and Mags had gone to the bar but they seemed to be having an argument with the barman. Obviously, he had seen how young me and Kev were and was refusing to serve them; but then he raised his voice and I heard him say, "No! She is not drinking in my pub. Not looking like that."

There was an animated discussion between Gary and Mags and then she turned around and walked straight out of the pub. Gary came towards us balancing three pints of beer in his hands and we went to a small table in the corner; me and Kev sat with our backs to the bar. I told Gary it was terrible that Mags was thrown out because of the way she was dressed.

Gary did not seem to have much sympathy: "Billy, her make-up made her look like a vampire, she was wearing a t-shirt with 'Filth' written on it, fishnet tights with more holes than they're supposed to have and she had Dr Martens on. Look at the blokes in here – she didn't exactly fit in. Besides, she don't care: she hates these stuffy old pubs." At that moment, most of the customers started getting up and going through a door at the back of the pub.

"Where is everyone going?" Kev asked his brother.

"Stripper. One of the great things about going to the pub at Sunday lunchtime. I'm having some; you two stay here, you're too young." With that, Gary, disappeared into the back bar.

I asked Kev if he did not think it odd that a pub, that threw out a woman because her clothes were too revealing, was happy to provide entertainment that involved a woman taking all her clothes off.

He did. "Hypocritical, Billy. It's hypocritical."

I also found it strange that Gary knew someone like Mags. In fact, I found Gary's enthusiasm for punk music unlikely but Kev said he loved how loud and fast it was and it was Mags who had got him into it in the first place. She was someone he had known for a long time, since before she was a punk. She was at art college now and the Sex Pistols had played there and she told Gary about them ages ago.

"Why does Gary not dress like a punk, then," I wondered.

"Too fat," Kev sniggered. "He thinks you have to be skinny to be a punk; and he's probably right."

Just then Gary bowled back into the bar with three more pints of beer. I was not enjoying drinking it: it tasted of soap and coffee and I had already been to the toilet once and wanted to go again. By the time we had a third, which Gary made me pay for because I had birthday money, I was tired and glad we were going home.

Falling out of the pub into the shock of the cold daylight, I had a sense that I had been doing something subversive. Drinking underage in a shady pub just off Petticoat Lane market, I felt like Winston Smith when he wandered down forbidden labyrinthine streets into the proles' district in *Nineteen Eighty-Four*. What I really felt was drunk; not in the insensible, painful way I had been on the Holy Land trip but in a pleasant way: warm and happy – but in desperate need of the toilet again.

Before the bus came Gary and Kev went down an alley and pissed up against the wall but I was too scared in case someone saw me. As soon as we were on the bus, I regretted it: my bladder felt like a slowly inflating balloon inside of me and the urge to wet myself and have done with it was almost irresistible. I decided I would have to get off and find a toilet and wait for another bus. At the next stop, as I told Kev what I was going to do, the driver turned off the engine.

"Why have we stopped?" I asked Kev.

"We're at the bus garage; they're changing drivers. You've got time to go and have a piss and get back on again."

Giving Kev my stuff to hold, I ran down the stairs and jumped off the bus. The driver and conductor were walking away but there was no sign of their replacements. I had time. There was an alley next to the bus garage but it had a gate across it. I tried to open it but it was locked so I scrambled up and dropped down on the other side. The feeling of relief when I started was heavenly and I was engulfed in a rising crowd of steam from the torrent of piss. I was just beginning to wonder if it would ever end when a door opened further down the alley and a bus crew came out and started walking towards me. Unable to stop what I was doing, I tried to hide my dignity and blend into the wall.

"You disgusting little bastard," one of them said as they passed.

"Filth," the other agreed.

They opened the gate and went towards the bus - but they left it wide open. I looked up. I could see Kev and Gary pointing and laughing at me. Their hilarity alerted others and very soon the whole top deck was laughing their heads off watching me piss. Even worse, at the front of the bus I could see Colin Cummings and two other kids from the school trip grinning down at me. Worse still, I was just finishing when I heard the bus engine come to life and two sharp rings of the bell. The bus began to pull away and, doing up my flies, I started running after it with a crowd of howling faces pressed against the upper windows. Being a fast runner, I easily caught up and I grabbed the rail and leapt on to the platform. When I emerged at the top of the stairs the passengers all looked round and gave me a little cheer. I felt such a fool. When I sat down, Kev gave me that pitying sigh and shake of the head. "You are priceless, Billy."

The stop before ours, Colin Cummings and his mates got up to get off. Cummings stopped when he reached our seats. "Still acting the clown, Monson? Listen, I'm having a party next month: a sort of reunion for everyone who went on the trip. Some of those private school girls from Kent are coming. I think that girl Sophie that you made a prat of yourself over in assembly is one of them. You should come. At least you'll be entertaining." With that, he disappeared downstairs. Sophie. I was going to see Sophie again. I felt terrified.

At home, Dad had cooked Sunday dinner and he had saved me some; the meat was a bit dried up and the gravy had congealed but I was hungry. With time for it to sink in, the terror of seeing Sophie again had turned into excitement. It meant I had two parties to go to: first Deborah and Mole's flat-warming and then the reunion. I thought of Dad's saying about waiting ages for a bus and then two coming along together.

"You look happy, Billy. Had a good time this morning?"

"Yes. I got some good stuff. And I just heard some great news, too."

I knew Dad would not ask me what the news was and I was not going to tell him anything about Sophie. I had still not let on that I knew he had spent Christmas with Tina Breakspear's mum and he

23

had made no attempt to tell me himself. We never spoke about anything important, certainly not feelings. Dad got nervous if conversation with me strayed too far from football or school. I think he was worried that I would want to talk about Mum, which I never did.

"Right. Good. Here, look. Have this. Birthday treat."

It was a pint of Dad's home brewed beer. I groaned inside and, because I did not want to hurt his feelings, poured most of it down the sink when he was out of the room.

MARCH

"Have you got a job as a chippy, or something?"

I had no idea what Dad meant but he was looking at my new trousers.

"You've got carpenter's jeans on. A bit tight, though. I suppose it's the fashion is it?"

I mumbled in agreement and went back to my room to get some LPs for Deborah's party. I was definitely taking the Ramones record, even though I knew there would be no one there who would appreciate it: they were too old, especially Mole. But I had to take some David Bowie, too. I might have started to listen to some different music but my loyalty to Bowie was as strong as ever: When everyone declared their allegiances at primary school, I had started off as a Marc Bolan fan and then moved to the Bowie group. I thought there was something embarrassing about other kids choosing Slade and Sweet: those groups had no elegance or grace; they were like blokes from the pub in fancy dress and glittery faces. They had disappeared from the charts, now, and had been replaced by even worse groups, like The Rubettes and Sailor. Bolan was still just about hanging on and Bowie had faded a little, although he was back in the top 10, now.

I had always been aware of him even before Deborah set me on the right path. There had been the disconcerting Space Oddity - the astronaut being stranded in space disturbed me when I was little - and then the confusing lyrics to John I'm Only Dancing. Why was he apologising to John for dancing with a girl? Who was John to him? My ten-year-old mind could simply not understand it; I understood it now, of course, and I had stuck with him even though being a Bowie fan sometimes got you called queer at secondary school. Kev had once been in the Bowie camp but he had deserted for the safer ground of hard rock and Status Quo and stuff like that. Bowie's music was like home to me: it was always there. I decided to take *Low* to the party, now that Sound and Vision was a hit single, and *Young Americans* because Deborah liked it but Mole hated it. I wrote my name in the corner of the inner sleeve of all three LPs and put them in the Roy's Records carrier bag.

Although Deborah did not live too far away – at the end of the next estate - I was not looking forward to going there. The flat was in a tower block that the council called 'hard to let'. Mole said that meant the people who lived there were hard and the police let them do what they want. That was why they had got the flat so quickly. Dad said they should wait for an offer of somewhere better but Deborah was keen to move. I think she felt that this would be the last time she would leave home now that she had a council tenancy of her own. Little Michael was still here, though; we had looked after him while they moved and he was staying over until after the party. I thought Dad would not be happy, having to stay in and look after him on a Saturday night, but he seemed in an unusually good mood.

The light was fading when I left home but I preferred to walk. You never knew who you might meet on a bus at night; at least in the street you could run away from any trouble. I walked the route that Mole had driven in his old van when I helped him move some of their stuff the previous evening. That way, I could come to their block from the other direction and not have to walk through the whole estate. It might take longer but it was worth it if it meant I could stick to the roads. It was a mild evening but it had been raining and the streets were quiet. I hardly saw anyone the whole way there but, as the tower block came into view, I could make out a huddle of bodies sitting down in the children's play area near the entrance. Occasional clouds of smoke rose above their heads and I could hear the deep murmur of their voices; they looked like a group of old men who should have been conspiring in a pub rather than in the open air. I would have to walk right past them so I hung back at the edge of the road waiting for a sudden burst of bravery. Or for them to leave.

After a few minutes they showed no sign of moving and some people were coming up the road behind me so I decided to walk very quickly, across the grass, to the tower block entrance. As I passed the playground I sensed that one of the huddle looked up. They had.

"Oi! Roy! What records you got then?" It was not an old voice but someone about my age and it had an edge of menace.

"Fucking hell. Look at his strides. He looks like Max Wall." Another voice, a little older, a lot colder.

I kept walking and looking straight ahead to try and ignore them, but I could hear movement and footsteps so I started to run for the entrance. I scooted through the door, past the lift - it had not been working the day before - and up the stairs, taking two at a time. I had no idea if they were coming after me or not but I kept going at the same pace until I reached the tenth floor. I had a stitch and the backs of my legs were killing me. I hammered on Deborah's door.

"Alright, alright!" Mole appeared. "Blimey, you're keen, man."

I nearly knocked him over as I dashed inside, breathless. I was not sure that this being different was such a good idea. Deborah was still getting ready in the bathroom and Mole was in the front room with the only other two people already at the party. They were smoking and talking and Pink Floyd were on the record player. I realised that the wallpaper was the same as in our hallway at home. Council wallpaper. I went out onto the balcony: the lights of London were burning brightly in front of me and I could see the Post Office Tower blinking in the distance. I looked down at the playground; there was no one there. I sat on a box in the kitchen waiting for things to get started. There was a table with drinks on it but no chairs. There was very little furniture anywhere in the flat: there were only beds in the bedrooms and there was a settee in the front room, some cushions on the floor and a coffee table with the record player on it. The rooms seemed bigger than at home but that could have just been the lack of furniture.

When Deborah emerged from the bathroom she seemed flustered: fussing over how much beer there was, wondering whether they should have bought some food. Mole told her not to worry: people just wanted to get pissed and they would bring booze as well.

When people started to arrive, I noticed that a lot of the women were girls Deborah had been to school with. By the way she greeted them, she clearly had not seen some of them for a while. Some of them had boyfriends with them and I recognised a couple from football. A few blokes were obviously Mole's mates: they looked as scruffy as him. There was no one of my age so I was treated like a pet: fussed over by the women; given a few sips of beer by the men; had the mickey taken out of my trousers by both.

I managed to get my Ramones LP played for a little while but no one seemed to be aware of it and then someone took it off. I went and put it back in its sleeve and, when Earth Wind and Fire had finished, I slipped *Low* on to the turntable; but once Sound and Vision had finished that got taken off, too, so I gave up. I took a can of beer from the kitchen and went and sat in the dark in little Michael's bedroom. I was supposed to be sleeping in Michael's bed for the night but I was bored and I wanted to go home. I could hear the sound of *Young Americans* so I knew Deborah was in control of the records. After a while, a couple came in and started snogging up against the wall. They failed to notice me and I started to panic in case they moved on to something else. It was only when I got up that they saw me. I rushed to the door and opened it; in the shaft of light I realised the man was Mole but the woman was not my sister.

I was nervous about going home on my own because of the reception committee that had greeted me when I arrived but I definitely wanted to leave now. I started looking for Deborah to tell her. I was peering into the gloom of the front room when I heard my name being called. It was Gary. Of course, he was the same age as my sister. He was sitting on the floor in the corner with Mags. She looked bored.

"Wotcha, Billy boy. Them trousers are looking good, eh Mags?"

"Yeah, but you still need to sort the rest of it out. That white t-shirt's alright, though it's a bit plain. It's the training shoes and the hair."

How did Mags know what to wear? I had considered writing 'Ramones' or 'Sex Pistols' on my t-shirt but I thought it would look stupid. I did not have enough money to get monkey boots and I had no idea where to buy plastic sandals. I had remembered the Woolworth's baseball boots that I used to wear when I was little: they still sold them and I thought I might get a pair. They looked a bit like what the Ramones were wearing on the cover of their LP.

"I'll cut your hair, if you like? I've done some of my friends' and I did my own." Mags' hair was dyed jet black, spiky on top, a jagged fringe at the front and straggly wisps hanging down at the back. "Let's do it now."

I did not answer but when she got up I followed her to the kitchen. She found some scissors in a drawer and we went to the bathroom. I sat on the toilet seat while she started to cut. My hair was not that long but I was alarmed at how much of it was landing in my lap and on the floor; but I was also excited at the transformation I was undergoing. Mags cut a lot from the back and I could sense the cool air of the bathroom on my exposed neck. It felt liberating. She disappeared for a while and came back with some beer and a comb. She worked in silence, teasing up the hair on the top of my head with the comb and clipping each clump with the kitchen scissors. When she had finished cutting, she lathered up some soap in her hands and worked it through my hair. She stood back and admired her creation then led me to the mirror above the sink. I gasped: my hair was short and spiky all over. I looked like another person. I looked like the bloke from The Clash who had talked about his mates working in factories. Dad was going to kill me.

We went back to the front room to find Gary but he was not there. It was dark so nobody noticed my hair. We went to the kitchen: under the fluorescent strip light, everybody noticed my hair. Gary was talking to Deborah but they stopped dead when they saw me. Gary laughed his approval but Deborah's face fell. "Dad'll kill me. I'll get the blame for this."

Two of her old schoolfriends tried to calm her down but I think she was drunk because she started crying. They took her off to the bathroom and Gary went to find Mole to tell him. When he came back he said him and Mags were leaving. I told them to wait for me. The bathroom was empty so I went to the front room. Everyone was dancing to Heatwave and I could see Deborah in the middle of them waving her hands above her head. Boogie Nights. Disco shit, Kev would say. I decided not to tell her I was going home and gathered up my LPs. I ignored Mole as I passed him in the hall and followed Gary and Mags out of the flat.

It was not late but I felt safer walking through the streets with them: big, tough Gary in front, me and Mags behind – two punks together. I also felt special: twice, cars sounded their horns at us.

Mags gave them a V-sign and said it always happened to her because she was a punk. "You'll have to get used to it."

My much less hairy head was cold in the night air but it was a reminder that I was changed – I was like a new person, I had been born again. Although I was angry about what I had seen at the party, and had no idea what to do about it, I just did not care. Deborah and Mole could get on with their own stupid lives. I worried about little Michael, though. We walked all the way to my block even though they were going to catch a bus to the West End. Mags said I should come with them; I was tempted because Dad was not expecting me home but Gary said I was too young and he did not want to be responsible for me.

"Next time," Mags said. "You've got to come and see one of the groups with us."

When I got into the hall, I could see a light under the front room door and I could hear music. Dad rarely played records and what I heard was unfamiliar to me. I went and opened the door of Deborah's old bedroom; little Michael was sleeping soundly. As I quietly closed it, I heard the front room door open behind me.

"Why are you home?"

I turned around. Dad looked angry. "I was bored at the party."

"What the bloody hell have you done to your hair?"

I wanted to ask Dad what he had done to his mouth because it looked as though it was smeared with strawberry jam; but then I looked past him into the front room and I could see Tina Breakspear's mum's bright red lips as she turned to look at me from low down on the settee. I ignored Dad's questions and went to my room.

I got sent to old Burkett's office on Monday morning because of my hair. He told me that I should not return to school the next day with it still "sticking up like a bog brush." In the meantime, I became such a curiosity that Simmons took me to the library at break to get away from all the boys who wanted to look at or - worse - touch my hair.

I walked home with Kev after school and we went to his flat. He seemed to be slightly in awe of the fact I had let Mags cut my hair.

There seemed to be a difference in the way he talked to me; he was treating me like an equal. Kev was much cleverer than me and that showed in the way he usually dealt with me; he did not do it to be nasty – he just took the lead all the time. I let him do it because it seemed natural: he was in the upper stream at school and I was in the middle stream, and even then, he was at the top of most his classes and I was near the bottom of most of mine; there was a gulf between us. The only subject I did well in was English, which was Kev's weakest. I was good at English because I enjoyed reading but also because I liked my teacher, Miss Kelly. She was one of the few female teachers in the school and the only one who called me by my first name. I was also quite good at Art but Kev did Technical Drawing, instead. He said English and Art were no use to you if you wanted to get a good job. That was fine by me: I was not interested in any sort of job – good or bad.

We listened to Kev's three punk singles and then a song by The Clash that Kev had taped with his cassette recorder from the John Peel programme on the radio. It was called White Riot and was really fast and just as exciting as the Sex Pistols. It was hard to understand what the singer was saying but I did catch some words about school teaching you to be thick and power being in the hands of rich people. It sounded so angry. School and rich people. They were good things to be angry about.

Kev went and got some of his brother's music papers. I used to buy them sometimes to find out what David Bowie was doing but there were only ever dull articles about Black Sabbath and Deep Purple, so I gave up; but in the latest, there were some pieces about the punk groups – I made a note to buy them again when I could afford to. I found out that the singer in The Clash was called Joe Strummer, which made me laugh because the guitars sounded nothing like they were being strummed. There was a picture of Johnny Rotten: he was wearing an old sixties suit jacket like Dad had in the back of his wardrobe, but it was tatty and he had stuck pins in the lapels and was wearing a medal. His open face was staring hard into the camera; he looked angelic and demonic at the same time.

Kev's mum asked me to stay so I had my tea there. Kev's dad took the mickey out of my hair but Gary defended me saying at least

31

I had the guts to be a bit different. I walked home feeling good because of that but also because it was only five days until the reunion when I would see Sophie. We had started reading *Romeo and Juliet* in English and, even though it was difficult to understand, my interest was piqued because the main character was lovesick over a girl and he was going to a masked ball just so he could see her; it seemed like a good omen. However, he was in love with a different girl from the one in the title, which made me apprehensive about what might happen. Overall, though, the prospect of the party was one that thrilled me. In my cheerful mood, even the estate looked good: it was a warm evening and still light and kids were out on their bikes and people were outside their front doors leaning on the landing walls looking down into the courtyards. It felt as though winter was finally ending. When I got back to my block, I saw Tina Breakspear coming out of the stairwell with a girl I had never seen before. I put my head down but Tina called out, "I like your hair, Billy." I felt my face go as red as her mum's lips.

The door was opened by Colin Cummings' mum and dad. At least that is who I assumed they were but they introduced themselves to me as Caroline and Peter and that is what Cummings called them to their faces. However, it was very clearly their home, as they were being busy hosts and they seemed to know where everything was. I was a bit suspicious of how many personal questions they were asking me but I took it to be friendliness rather than nosiness. They looked and spoke like teachers.

"I do like your outfit, Billy," Caroline had said to me when I was standing in the hallway. My 'outfit' had been developed in the past week: I had bought a pair of baseball boots − or 'bumper boots' as Mum used to call them - from Woolworth's and I was wearing Dad's old suit jacket. Best, though, was my t-shirt: I had written 'The Clash' on the front in felt pen, in the slashed way it was written in a music paper advertisement for their White Riot single. And having spent the week at school trying to keep my hair flat, I had used some soap on it, the way Mags had, to make it spiky again.

Cummings took me through to the front room. Caroline had called it the sitting room so, as soon as I found a space, I thought I had better sit down. There were about fifteen boys in the room and they were drinking beer. They were all upper stream fourth of fifth years but not all of them had been on the trip. There was no sign of Sophie or any girls.

"Look everyone, Monson is a punk," Cummings sneered. They all looked at me.

"Have you brought any punk records with you?" one of them asked.

I almost regretted that I had left the Ramones LP at home but I had decided not to bring any records, as I felt I could not trust Cummings and his crowd with them.

Peter came in and gave me a small can of beer. I stayed sitting down while the others milled about looking at LP covers and singing along to the record that was playing. It was a rock record but not hard rock; it was not something I recognised. The sitting room was huge: it went all the way from the front of the house to the back and the ceiling was high. When Nan and Grandad were alive, they had lived in a house like this before they moved to their warden-assisted flat; but they had two small separate rooms where the Cummings had one; and the way it was decorated was nothing like Nan and Grandad's. There was no wallpaper: instead, the walls were painted plain white and there were paintings hanging on them. The paintings were mostly abstract: I had painted a few abstract pictures at school but I felt they never came out right; these looked so striking. The furniture was all white, as well, and there was a shaggy white rug in the middle of the floor. There was a table with food on at the back that was made of metal and glass. The only bright colours in the room came from the paintings and an unpatterned orange carpet.

The longer the party went on with no sign of Sophie, the more I was convinced that she was not coming – that no girls were coming. The boy who asked me if I had brought any punk records sat down next to me on the settee. He had not been on the trip but I knew he was a friend of Cummings from school called Nick Phillips.

He turned to me. "Why are you here?"

"Because I was invited," I replied.

"But why were you invited? You're very out of place here, don't you think?"

He was right. Almost all the other boys looked the same with their shoulder-length centre-parted hair and denim flares; but I was not about to give him the satisfaction of letting him know that I felt uncomfortable. I was bolstered by the can of beer. "I went on the Holy Land trip. Why are you here?"

He was momentarily unsettled but then regained his composure: he feigned a yawn, stretched his arms above his head and smiled. "I'm here to help out with the girls."

Despite the urge to call him a wanker it at least confirmed to me that the girls were expected. I got up to get away from him and went to look for the toilet. In Nan and Grandad's house, there was one at the end of the kitchen so I walked down the hallway and opened the kitchen door. Caroline and Peter were in there with two other adults, drinking wine and laughing.

"What can we do for you, Billy?"

I was surprised she had remembered my name. "I'm looking for the toilet."

"Upstairs on the right on the first landing. You can't miss it, darling."

Up the stairs there were rugs in bright colours that looked as though they were from India; but they were on the wall rather than on the floor. On a table at the top of the stairs an incense stick was burning; the smell was sweet and soothing. I was puzzled that Cummings was such a tosser when he had such pleasant parents and lived in a large, comfortable house.

When I was in the bathroom, I heard car doors slamming in the street followed by a knock on the door. Then I heard lots of excited chatter in the hallway and the voices were distinctly female; the girls had arrived. I felt sick. When I went downstairs I would see Sophie again. I sat down on the edge of the bath to stop myself from breathing so fast.

When I was coming back down the stairs, there was a gaggle of parents in the hall below me introducing themselves to Caroline and Peter. Peter was shaking hands and taking coats from people and Caroline was talking to them in the same inquisitive but friendly way she had spoken to me. I heard some of their names – Robert and Elizabeth, David and Frances, James and Penelope – and I could see

34

that they all looked just like their hosts. As they headed for the kitchen, I made my way back into the sitting room.

It was now very crowded as there were about a dozen girls amongst the boys. I stood just inside the doorway looking around the room to see if I could spot Sophie but she did not seem to be there. I started to move through the throng and some of the girls gave me strange looks as I squeezed past. And then I saw Sophie. She was at the back of the room. She was laughing and, as she threw back her head, her long dark hair tumbled down her back. In the build-up to each laugh she wrinkled her nose and looked to the side. She was beautiful.

The only problem was that she was talking to Nick Phillips and showed no sign of moving away from him. What I had not considered, in all my anticipation of the moment, was that I would have to summon up the courage to approach Sophie. In my head, I had imagined that she would simply scoot up to me, link her arm through mine and we would restart our relationship where we left off on the cruise ship.

I hovered around the food table for what seemed like an age waiting for a chance to talk to her. I was sure that everyone was watching me, that the whole party hinged on whether I would have the guts to go and talk to a girl; but when I looked around, they were all too busy talking and laughing amongst themselves to notice my torment.

In need of something to give me more nerve, I went to the kitchen and asked if I could have another can of beer. Caroline gave me a look of mock disapproval but the booze was clearly being rationed; Peter reluctantly gave me another can and I went back and stood leaning against the wall in the sitting room and drank the can quickly. Sophie was still talking to Phillips and they seemed to be standing closer together than they had been before.

When I could bear it no longer, I walked up to them; they both turned around to look at me at the same time and, as they did so, I blurted out Sophie's name. Before she even uttered her reply, I knew where we stood - I read everything in her look: the slight widening of the eyes in surprise, the barely perceptible glance that took in my shape from my soap-spiked hair down to my cheap kids' shoes, the frozen smile that spread across her face.

"Hi," she said, raising her hand with the palm faced towards me in a subconscious halting gesture. Then she turned back to Phillips and continued talking.

I did not know whether it was the change in my appearance that had prompted her reaction to me or the fact that I was just one of many barely-remembered people she had met on the trip. Whether anything that had existed between us had been real or simply imagined by me was irrelevant now. Whatever relationship we might have had was now certainly one that we would never have. I was in a room with thirty people that I had no connection with at all, at a party I should never have gone to. Phillips was right, I was very out of place. I made my way back across the sitting room, into the hallway, out through the front door and left another party early.

APRIL

"You're going out with Tina Breakspear?"

It was Easter weekend and I was at football with Kev. The match was very dull, so we had decided to beat the rush by going for pies before half-time; but so had everyone else and we were in the usual long queue. I had not told him about my humiliation at Cummings' reunion party but I had mentioned that Tina's mum and my dad were seeing a lot of each other. I had wondered out loud whether Tina knew about it and Kev said she did. When I asked him how he knew he said he knew because she was his girlfriend.

"How long has this been going on?"

Kev looked a little shamefaced. "Sort of since Christmas. We got together at the youth club Christmas disco but we've only been officially going out for the past few weeks."

"Is that how you knew my dad had gone away for Christmas - Tina told you?"

"Yeah. She doesn't care about her mum very much and isn't bothered what she does."

I had been worrying unnecessarily over what Tina might think. I was relieved that I could stop avoiding her, although it still might be awkward talking to her about it. I had thought that Dad carrying on with Tina's mum was a source of embarrassment for me, but my main worry was that, in other people's eyes, Dad looked like a fool.

Since I had been the inside the Cummings' house, I had been thinking about Dad a lot. Seeing a house like the one Nan and Grandad lived in – the house Dad grew up in – reminded me that in the few years before Mum died, Dad had lost his mum and then his dad. In my selfishness, I had forgotten just how much he had experienced. It was easy to forget. He never showed any sign that he was affected - he just plodded on through life: work, pub, football and, in between, doing his best by me with his bad cooking and making sure I did my homework. Whenever Deborah had come back to live with us he was probably quite glad: there was a bit more life in the flat with her and Mole and little Michael around. When it was just me and Dad, I would often be in my room and he would either be in the pub drinking or in the front room watching telly. At least when Deborah was at home, we ate much better food.

I had been thinking about Deborah, as well. I had not seen her since the flat-warming party and she was upset with me over my hair when I left. Dad was not happy about my hair but because I had caught him with Tina's mum, he felt he was in no position to moralise. He did tell me he had been reading about punk rockers in his newspaper with all their spitting and pogo dancing and he was not impressed. I was puzzled by Deborah's reaction because she had come back from her six months of squatting with an orange Bowie cut.

The reason I had kept away from Deborah's flat was not my hair but because I was at a loss to know what to do about Mole's behaviour at the party. I felt I should tell Deborah but I was worried what the consequences would be. If she and Mole split up, would her and little Michael stay in their hard to let flat or would they come back and live with me and Dad again? I was not sure which was worse: it upset me to think of the two of them fending for themselves in the that tower block but the upheaval every time Deborah came home was exhausting. The only consolation was that Mole would not be around.

The second half was no better and the match finished nil-nil. On the bus home Kev said that him and Tina were going to her cousin's youth club in Bromley one night in the week and that I should go with them. He said her cousin wanted to get into punk; she had seen me and liked my hair and had asked Tina if I would come along. I realised that she must have been the other girl when I saw Tina outside our block a few weeks earlier. I felt as though I was being set-up so I said to Kev I was not sure and I would let him know. If a girl was interested in me that was good; but I was not willing to bear any more disappointment so I told myself that she probably just wanted to meet more like-minded people.

When I got home, Dad was not back from the match. I went to my room and put on the new Clash LP. I had asked Dad for some money for Easter, as I was getting too old for chocolate eggs, and me and Kev had been to the record shop in the High Street that morning and bought a copy each. It had all changed in the shop: The Clash LP had been on display in the window and a young bloke served us; he said we had good taste and it was the best LP for ages.

As I had the flat to myself, I turned the volume up loud and wandered from room to room as I listened to it for the first time. The songs sounded so urgent and aggressive; one called London's Burning was about how boring everything was because people sat around watching the telly. Another song, called Career Opportunities, was about not wanting to do jobs other people wanted you to do; it reminded me of what one of the group had said about his mates from school all working in factories. I played the LP through three times. It made me want to rush outside and tell people to come and listen but they would all be slumped on the settee watching Rolf Harris or Val Doonican; and it made me want to go out, to be less boring myself, to do something before I ended up with a narrow life working in the biscuit factory, like Dad.

I was nervous about going to a youth club in a different area – I didn't even go to the one on our estate – but Bromley was in the suburbs and I was sure it must be better than where I lived. And I knew two good things about Bromley. Firstly, it was where David Bowie grew up and, secondly, I had read in *Sounds* about a group of people called the Bromley Contingent who were the first fans of the Sex Pistols; if people there liked the Sex Pistols then they would surely welcome my spiky hair and hand-drawn t-shirt. Kev and Tina were very relaxed and said it would be fine; Kev even had his punk singles with him to play. Tina said she had been to Bromley a lot, because her mum lived there with her aunt, and it was a very quiet place and there was never any aggro.

On the bus, Tina said to me that she was as embarrassed as I was by her mum and my dad carrying on but we had no need to worry about it. "It's not as though we're all going to move in together, is it?" she laughed.

This was not something I had even considered. Tina was not living with her mum so she would be unaffected by any plans they might have but I was living with my dad. I felt alarmed by the prospect of a change as serious as that.

As the bus got nearer to Bromley the buildings became smaller: the tower blocks disappeared and then the low-rise flats began to peter out to be replaced by streets of identical houses. It appeared less threatening and harsh but somehow more dreary and dull; and by the time we got off the bus, I felt quite deflated by how unexciting the place looked. We left the main road and walked down several narrow streets until we came to a small children's playground and, next to it, a long, low brick building. It had metal grilles over the windows and looked just like the youth club on our estate.

Inside, there was a small hall where some kids were playing table tennis and others were sitting around the edges on plastic chairs, chatting. We walked up a corridor to the back. Halfway along, a door flew open and a boy and a girl fell out, laughing; the room behind them was in darkness except for the flickering light of a TV screen. The end of the corridor opened out into a slightly larger hall that had some chairs and a hatch serving drinks at the near end; there was a record player on a table at the far end and some girls were in front of it dancing to Abba.

I looked around the hall. There was no sign of the Bromley Contingent or anyone who looked remotely like me and Kev. There was something very underwhelming about the place: nobody looked like they were having a good time; even the dancers looked miserable, shuffling about from foot to foot.

Tina's cousin, Lorraine, came up to us. She smiled at me and said hello, but I could tell she was not interested in me. We all sat down and had some Coca Cola and crisps. Lorraine looked at Kev's singles and said we would be able to play them soon. She took them down to the other end of the hall and left them on the table by the record player in a sort of queue. I was glad I had not brought any of my records.

Gradually, the hall filled up and the lights were turned down and the music was turned up. Play That Funky Music by Wild Cherry was put on and the dancing became a little livelier. Lorraine went down to the record player with Kev and then the Sex Pistols single came on; the dancers all moved to the side of the hall. Kev came back.

"We've got to dance," he said to me through gritted teeth.

"What?"

Lorraine came back. "Come on, Billy. Everyone's expecting you and Kev to show us that pogo dancing."

This was awful. I could sense the colour draining from my face and I felt faint. Lorraine started pulling me out of my chair. I was not sure my legs would support me.

"Come on. It'll be a laugh. I'll join in."

She dragged me to the other end of the hall. Kev was ahead of me and when he turned around he looked as though he was trying to make himself physically smaller; he was hunched over and looking at the floor. Lorraine had hold of both of my hands; I tried to pull away, but she held on and started jumping up and down in front of me, laughing. I was beginning to hate Lorraine. We were engaged in a tug of war and I was losing. As this spectacle went on, I thought that the longer I protested, the more I was drawing attention to myself; eventually, I joined in. Lorraine started to turn us around and around and I could see the faces of the retired dancers behind her as we rotated: their expressions were uncomprehending. I kept catching glimpses of Kev as we spun: he seemed to be lolloping about, mimicking a small child's impersonation of a hopping frog. Tina was nowhere to be seen. I had not realised before how long Anarchy in the UK was; it seemed to go on forever. I got the impression that everyone in the youth club had now gathered to watch us. When I could bear it no longer, I wrenched myself free of Lorraine's grasp and, with the intention of really giving them something to stare at, began frantically leaping about on my own like a caught fish twitching on the end of a line. I sensed that Lorraine and Kev had both stopped and I was the centre of attention. I kept going until Johnny Rotten's final snarl of "destroy!", and then I stopped. I stood there looking at the circle of blank faces; the blank faces stared back at me; the hall was completely silent. Then someone moved and changed the records over and the sound of Rose Royce brought the dancers back to life. They drifted around me and resumed their shuffling.

We went and sat down again. Tina was laughing so hard that she could barely catch her breath. Lorraine said what a laugh it was, but Kev looked suicidal.

"That was the worst experience of my life."

"Oh, shut up, Kev," Tina chided him, "it was funny. You should have seen everyone's faces. They've never seen anything like it. And Billy was brilliant. He looked crazy. You should've done what he did."

I was not even sure I should have done what I did, but at least I gave the impression that I did not care what people thought of me. And, in a way, I was past caring what anyone thought of me. Who were those morons to pass judgement on me, dancing like showroom dummies to their boring, crappy records?

A boy came over to me and tapped me on the arm. "See him over there?" He pointed at another boy leaning against the wall halfway down the hall. He was about the same age as me; he had a low forehead and a cruel face. His thick arms hung limply by his side.

"Yes, I can see him. What about him?"

"He's going to give you a kicking afterwards."

With that, he turned away and walked back over to the boy he had pointed out. They both stood leaning against the wall, looking over at me.

"What have I done?" I said to Lorraine.

"Oh, those two. They're always looking for a fight. It's the same every week. They always have to find someone to pick on. They haven't had a good evening unless they start something."

"What should I do?"

"They're idiots but it's probably best to leave a bit before the end. Don't hang around outside after."

This was not the reassurance I was hoping for. I looked over at the boys. The one who spoke to me was quite small, but the other was broad and his massive hands looked like bunches of bananas.

Kev said we should probably leave now but I was worried that they would simply follow us as soon we got up. "Let's go out one at a time," I suggested.

Kev agreed and I went first. Without looking at the two boys, I left the hall and walked down the corridor towards the front doors. When I got outside, I looked back in to see if Kev and Tina were following; they were not. Instead, the two boys were walking quickly down the corridor, Bunches in front and his little sidekick behind. I knew I had to take care of myself, so I started to run. I heard the doors burst open behind me and the boys' running feet. I put my head down and sprinted as fast as I could. I was not sure where I was going - I just ran. One identical street led into another and another and then I saw the main road up ahead of me. As I turned into it, I glanced back and could see two figures in the distance. There was no way I could wait at the bus stop, so I kept running along the main road. After a while, I stopped to look back; I could see people in the distance but they did not seem to be moving quickly so I doubted that they were my pursuers. Although I had outpaced them, I did not slow down until I reached a bus stop that I thought it was a good distance away from the youth club. Despite the quiet of the streets, I would not be happy until I was safely on the bus home. Soon after, I saw the comforting glow of an approaching block of light in the distance. When the bus pulled up, I sat inside rather than taking the chance of going upstairs. As soon as the bus pulled away, I heard footsteps above and the sound of two people coming downstairs. I was afraid to look but I sensed that they had sat down right behind me. Then there was an urgent tap on my shoulder and as I glanced round Kev and Tina burst out laughing.

"We had you going there, Billy!"

"You silly sods. I thought it was those boys."

"That's what we wanted you to think."

"Thanks a lot." Sometimes I had to remind myself that Kev was supposed to be my friend. "Why did that Bunches kid want to kick my head in?

"His name's Darren," Tina corrected me. "Basically, because you're a punk; and also, he really likes Lorraine and he probably thought you two were going out."

"I'd only just met her!"

"Yeah, but you were dancing with her."

I hardly thought that doing ring a ring a' roses constituted dancing together but I could see how it might have looked to a hardnut like Bunches. And Kev said being a punk could not have been the reason because, if it was, they would have started on him, too. I wanted to say it would have been difficult for them to tell that he was a punk: apart from his straight-leg jeans, Kev still looked like he always had.

"Well, you would have to be an idiot to want to beat someone up because they look different to you," I said instead.

I was glad to get back to our estate. Bromley was not that far away but it had felt like the end of the earth. I left Kev and Tina saying goodnight to each other in the courtyard and went up to the flat. Dad was making cheese on toast and I sat and had some with him in the kitchen. I did not mention what had happened; I just said it was fine when he asked me what the trip to the youth club was like. And it was fine. I had been scared when I was being chased but I was beginning to realise that narrow-minded people would struggle to accept what I was like: Deborah and Dad had; so had Cummings and his crowd; Sophie, as well; and ignorant morons like Bunches would react in the only way they could - by threatening violence. Mags was right: now my difference was visible, I would have to get used to it. I went to my room and listened to The Clash LP in the dark.

"I forgot. A girl called for you while you were out last night. Well, I say a girl – she looked more like a flippin' alien. She didn't say her name."

I thought Dad must be talking about Mags. "How old was she?"

"Hard to tell under all that weird make-up but probably a few years older than you. Who is she?"

"She's a friend."

"Some funny friends you've got these days, Billy."

"She's Gary's sort of girlfriend."

"Oh, Gary? I like Gary. Haven't seen him for a while. Is he alright?"

"He's just the same."

Later in the morning Kev appeared at the door. He had a new haircut. It was similar to mine but slightly longer. Only Mags could have cut it like that. He was grinning like mad and asked me what I thought. I said it was brilliant and asked him when he had it done. He said Mags was at his place when he got back from the youth club and she had done it then. I felt as though Kev was with me, we were in this together – whatever 'this' was.

"There's a reason I've had it done, now. We're going out on Sunday night. With Gary and Mags. We're going to a punk club in the West End. They've been going to it a lot and they say the groups are amazing."

Sunday was the last day of the Easter holidays. Dad was not going to let me go out the night before the first day of school. I wished I had gone out with them after Deborah's party when Dad had not been expecting me home.

"I'll have to let you know, Kev. I'm not sure my dad will let me go."

"What do you mean? You've got to go. Say you're coming round to mine for the evening; he'll never know."

We got off the bus at Waterloo and crossed the Thames on the footbridge by the Festival Hall. It was warm like a summer evening and people were strolling by the river. The light was fading and there were a few pleasure cruisers lazily navigating the current, their lights twinkling in the twilight. Despite the fact I was deceiving Dad, I had an overwhelming feeling of excitement. We were like a gang, walking along, and lots of passers-by gave us quizzical looks. Kev was wearing one of his dad's old white shirts with a skinny black tie. On the shirt, he had written the names of some of the groups we had read about or heard on John Peel. I had updated my homemade Clash t-shirt by colouring in the name and adding drawings of the police from the back cover of their LP. Gary wanted to go to the pub but Mags insisted we go straight to the club. We crossed the Strand and walked up past the girders and glass of the deserted fruit and veg market standing eerie and silent behind a street-long fence of corrugated iron. Even though we were in the centre of London, it was as run-down and tired as some of the places where we lived.

I was not sure what I was expecting the club to look like but, from the outside, it was like a public toilet. It had a tiled front and there was no sign that it was a club except for a small board that had the names of some of the groups playing there; I recognised Generation X and Siouxsie and the Banshees. I was worried me and Kev might not be allowed in, as we were only fifteen, but the bloke on the door gave us barely a glance. I had very little money – I could not have asked Dad for any when I was only supposed to be at Kev's house – and after I had paid to get in I had just enough left to get the bus home.

When we got inside, there was a small bar area with some leather settees around the wall with people slumped on them chatting and laughing. Some of them looked incredible, especially the women: I was a little embarrassed because their clothes were quite revealing but I tried to act as casual as I could when one of them came up to Mags and started talking to her. Gary got some small cans of beer for us and we went down some stairs. The walls were covered in writing. A tall punk coming up stopped in front of me and held open my jacket. I thought he was going to rip it off my shoulders but he just nodded, smiled and said, "Nice t-shirt."

I was surprised when the sound of the music hit me, because it was not punk but reggae. The bottom of the stairs opened out into a tiny room with a stage at one end. There was a group on the stage but they were moving equipment about and had either just finished or not started playing yet; the deafening bass was coming from records being played by a bloke with dreadlocks at the other end of the room.

Gary and Mags kept going off and chatting to different people who they obviously knew; me and Kev just stayed in the corner with our cans of beer, observing. I was surprised how many people were not punks; there were quite a few blokes with long hair and some others were so normal they would not have looked out of place at the youth club in Bromley. The stage had emptied and a different group were plugging in guitars and hitting drums. I realised I had only ever seen groups playing on the telly, on Top of the Pops.

Mags came over and talked to us but we could not hear a word she was saying. She put her mouth right next to my ear. Her breath was warm and it made my head swim. "This group is X-Ray Spex. I saw them a fortnight ago. They're my favourite. You're gonna love them, Billy." X-Ray Spex; like the adverts on the Bazooka Joe bubble gum comic. It struck me that X seemed to be an important punk letter.

People started to move up to the stage and we pushed in with them. Mags was ahead of me and Kev; she was right at the front. I could not see Gary anywhere. Two women came on stage and stood

46

in front of the guitarists and drummer. One of the women had a saxophone and the other a microphone. They looked amazing: they both had on army hats with goggles and they were wearing shiny black clothes. The singer said something about little girls being seen and not heard and then shouted, "Up yours!" As soon as she had finished speaking, the group began playing. The guitars were fast and loud and the saxophone wailed at the same speed. I was used to hearing saxophones on Bowie records but they never sounded like this. Over the top of it all, the singer bellowed at the same pitch as the saxophone. It was wonderful.

People around me were jumping in unison and my feet were lifted from the floor each time by their force. Those at the front, including Mags, kept falling on to the stage and had to hold on to the equipment to pull themselves back up. The tall punk who had complimented me on my t-shirt appeared next to me, thrashing about wildly. When he saw me, he grabbed my lapels and I had no choice but to join in with his reeling and whirling. All the while, he was grinning at me with a demented look on his face. Kev had got to the front and was leaping around next to Mags. There was no sign of his hopping frog dance. They played eight or nine songs, nearly all at the same pace, and finished with the one they had started with. I was exhausted by the end of it.

"What did I tell you, Billy? Weren't they great?"

Mags was right. I had never witnessed anything like it. I felt part of something even though I did not know most of the people there. It was electrifying. It was so different from the atmosphere at the youth club. And the two women on stage were so confident but they were only the same age as Mags - and that was only a few years older than me and Kev. I asked Mags if they were her favourite group because it was fronted by females.

"You're a clever kid, Billy boy; and you're probably right. That's what's so great about coming here: we're all equal. You don't have to be a bloke to be a punk or in a group. I can do whatever I want to do; you can do whatever you want to do."

When Mags said that, it made me think back to when I had watched the documentary about punk and the light that had come on in my head when one of The Clash talked about his mates working in factories. I was not going to do that; I was going to do whatever I wanted to.

We found Gary, who had been watching and listening from the back; he said he was too old for all that jumping around. He talked with Mags for a while and then he said to me and Kev that he needed to get us home. Mags stayed in the bar upstairs as we left. I did not understand Gary and Mags' relationship; I had never seen them kiss but they did seem to be very close. I asked Gary where Mags lived and he just said, "Here and there." I was feeling too elated to think what that might have meant.

My euphoria increased as we hit the cool night air outside. Seeing a group in action, hearing them play so loudly and urgently made the records I had been listening to sound tame in comparison. I felt as though everything had changed. How could me and Kev go to school the next day and act normally after that experience? As we walked back over the river to the bus stop, we chatted excitedly: about the music, what the group looked like, the other punks; and the reggae. A lot of the kids at school were into reggae and we heard it on our estate but it had never sounded as good as it did in the club. Kev said it had been the best night of his life. Gary laughed.

After we had got off the bus and walked to the estate, we went our separate ways. It was late and I thought Dad was probably going to have a go at me for not coming back from Kev's earlier. My excitement had died down a little and I was nervous as I put my key in the door. There was a light on in the hallway and the front room door was open but the telly was off. There was no sign of Dad. I went to his bedroom door; I hoped he was not in there with Tina's mum. I listened but could hear nothing. I tapped on the door but there was no answer so I opened it and looked in. His bed was empty. He was out. That was good, because he would have no idea when I had got home. Just as I was going into the bathroom, I heard his key in the lock. I looked back out. He looked flustered and angry.

"Alright, Dad? Have you been out?"

"Yes, I have. To Kev's - to find out where the bloody hell you'd got to, Billy."

MAY

As a result of my deception, Dad insisted that, until he could trust me again, I be at home by eight o'clock every evening. I had tried to explain to him that I had desperately wanted to go to the club and I knew he would not let me – that was why I had lied to him. I also said in mitigation that Kev had been allowed to go by his mum and dad and that Gary had been with us. He was not impressed by this and simply said that it was up to other people what they let their kids do but I was too young to be gallivanting around London at all hours. What amused me about Dad's clampdown was that I was very rarely out after eight. Recently there had been the two parties and the trip to the youth club but, ordinarily, I only ever went to Kev's or the football and neither of those kept me out late; and very often he was at the pub and had no idea whether I was home or not.

There was one positive outcome from what had happened. To try and get in Dad's good books I had got myself a Saturday job, so I had a bit of money; but there was also a devastating consequence of the new regime: Gary and Kev went to see The Clash play at a big theatre in North London and I was, of course, not allowed to go. There had been a riot in the audience and it had been reported in the newspapers. This only bolstered Dad's view that punk was a bad thing and lessened my chances of ever seeing a group again. Kev said that The Clash were incredible but it was not really a riot: some seats had got broken and people were actually passing them to the front to get them out of the way.

Perhaps even worse, was that Dad was making me do athletics. At parents evening, my PE teacher Mr McNally had said that I was a good runner and that I should join the athletics club he ran after school two days a week at the rec. McNally was a sadist and we were all afraid of him because getting on his wrong side could result in having a medicine ball dropped on your belly, being made to do press-ups in the mud or having a cold shower; but, at athletics club, he was completely different from the bullying character I knew in PE lessons. He never raised his voice, he laughed and he was encouraging. After I had tried different distances, he told me that my stamina was better than my pace and 1500 metres was my ideal race. I found the 1500 hard because it was almost four times around the track and I got knackered; but even though he was more approachable out of school, I was not going to disagree with him. I thought I had done best at 400 metres, coming second or third each time, but there was a kid in my year called Dennis White who always came first by a long way.

Apart from keeping me away from my bedroom and my records, the other downside of athletics club was that Colin Cummings and his mate, Nick Phillips, also went. The first time I had been there, Phillips shouted out, "I didn't know punk rockers could run!" but he was immediately silenced by a look of disapproval from McNally. I tried to keep out of their way as much as possible which was easy as, apart from warming up together, we usually separated to concentrate on our specialist events; Cummings and Phillips were high jumpers and 800 metre runners. I especially hated Phillips for his smarmy arrogance and because he had spent so long talking to Sophie at the party. I had, however, got Sophie out of my system. In fact, it had got to the point where I only ever thought about her when I saw him. She had turned out to be my Rosaline, not my Juliet; there was no Juliet.

The day Kev had been telling me all about seeing The Clash, I was in the changing room at the rec getting my kit on when Cummings and Phillips came in. When they saw me, they laughed and went to the other end of the room. They began a hushed conversation in which the only word they deliberately said loudly was 'Sophie'; I tried to act as though I could not hear them. Even as the changing room started to fill up, they carried on their joke and others looked at me and grinned each time Sophie's name was mentioned: everyone remembered me saying her name in assembly. Cummings and Phillips got louder and louder; they were almost shouting out her name and the other boys were raucously laughing. All the time, I kept my head down, tying the laces of my running shoes, until a louder voice made me look up.

"Why you picking on this boy?"

"It's, it's, it's just a joke," stammered Cummings.

"Well, it don't seem funny to me. Leave him alone."

The voice belonged to Dennis White and it silenced the changing room. Cummings and Phillips finished getting changed quickly and quietly and went out to the track. I felt embarrassed that I was unable to fight my own battles but I caught Dennis's eye and smiled my thanks; he coolly nodded in response and carried on getting changed. He was the same age as me but he seemed to be so much older: he was taller and broader and his voice was deep like a man's. I felt like a six-stone weakling in comparison.

After athletics club, I decided to do something I had been putting off for a while. I had not been to Deborah's flat since her party and, although she had come to see me and Dad with little Michael a couple of times, I kept out of their way as much as I could. Mole had not been with them, which was a blessing because I would have found it hard to look him in the face after what I had seen him doing. I hoped Mole would still be at work – if he was working – so I could tell my sister what he had been up to. My conscience had been wrestling with what to do, veering from thinking it was none of my business to feeling I had a responsibility to make sure my sister knew what Mole was like.

I was relieved to see that there were only small children in the play area next to Deborah's block: I had done enough running at athletics club. The lift still did not seem to be working so I trudged wearily up the stairs to the tenth floor. My sister eventually opened the door after shouting out to find out who it was.

I followed her to the kitchen and she put the kettle on. Since my last visit, a table and chairs had been added and, when I looked in the front room, there was more furniture in there than before. There was no sign of Mole. *Animal Magic* was on the telly and little Michael was playing with his toy cars in front of it. He jumped up when he saw me and told me it was his birthday soon.

"I can't believe he's nearly four," I said to Deborah back in the kitchen.

"I know. It's gone so quickly."

I sensed that it was going to be up to me to keep the conversation going. "The flat's looking nice."

"Well, yeah. It's amazing what you can get at those second-hand shops near the market."

Johnny Morris was doing the voices of the animals at the zoo. Deborah gave me a cup of tea and sat down.

"I'm glad Mole isn't here," I began, "because…"

She cut across me. "He's gone. I kicked him out a month ago. I was glad to see the back of him."

Deborah's tears at her party had been nothing to do with the haircut Mags had given me; she knew on the night that Mole had made a beeline for one of her old school friends. Gary had already told her having seen them out on the balcony. How was it that Gary instantly knew that the right thing to do was tell Deborah when it had taken me two months to come to the same conclusion? The same behaviour had been the cause of every break-up they had had; the reason for her very first return home was because Mole had gone off with another girl from the squat they were living in – even when Deborah was pregnant, he had let her down. I had no need to tell her what I had seen – it was merely a footnote in his history of cheating. I wanted to ask her if this meant she was coming back to live with me and Dad but, when she had finished talking, I simply asked, "What will you do now?"

"Stay here and carry on. Michael starts school in September and I'll be able to get a better job, then. I don't need Mole: he was like a child and I've already got one of those to look after."

I was relieved that she was staying in her flat but the thought of her and little Michael struggling on in a grim tower block, ten floors up with a lift that never worked, made me miserable. But Deborah did not seem sad; she had a determination about her and, despite an awkwardness between us at first, she had told me openly about her life with Mole in a way that she had never spoken to me before.

"What's going on with you, Billy? Dad tells me he's stopped you going out after you went to that punk rock club."

"Yes. And it's an open-ended sentence."

"But he's still letting you have your hair like that: it looks even worse."

To me, it looked better now than when Mags had cut it; but I could understand that the less enlightened would not view the

52

modifications I had been making with the kitchen scissors in a positive light. The spikiness had become less symmetrical and it had more of a hacked look which pleased me a lot; and I had been getting away without wearing it flat at school, although I had been getting quite a bit of abuse from other kids. I had also improved and expanded my wardrobe: inspired by pictures of The Clash, I had spattered paint on some of my t-shirts and trousers; and I now had more than one pair of trousers as I had spent hours with a needle and thread turning all my flares into straight legs, including my school trousers.

"And your trousers. You look like you're wearing bloody tights. Has Dad seen those?"

"No, I go to school after he's left for work and I'm back before he's home. I better go soon."

"What else are you up to?"

"I've got a job at the record shop on Saturday mornings. Just putting LP sleeves in the racks, opening boxes of records, that sort of stuff. And making tea for John, who runs it."

"It's a good job you don't serve the customers. You'll put them off looking like that."

The truth was, I think I got the job because I did look like that. John was the son of the grumpy git who used to run the shop and he wanted to bring it up to date. Fed up with asking Dad for money, I had surprised myself by going in and asking John for a job; more to my surprise, he had said yes. It was only four hours and I got paid £2; I got a discount on records and John had already given me a single by The Stranglers for free.

I told Deborah that I would come again soon and I got up to leave. She saw me to the door and then did something I could not remember her ever doing: she hugged me tightly and kissed me on the cheek.

It was the last day of the football season and Kev was waiting for me outside after I finished work so we could go to the match. I had spent most of the morning breaking up cardboard boxes out the back; I had hardly been in the shop, although during the short time I had been in there filing LP sleeves two boys I recognised from school

53

came in and bought the Clash LP. I told Kev I was fed up with breaking boxes but he ignored it and instead started talking about what him and Tina had done the previous night. He had not asked me anything about my job since I started it and I got the feeling he was either not interested or jealous. A few people shouted out at us as we walked through the market, but we were getting used to the attention our appearances attracted. We usually got a few comments at football but they were always humorous rather than aggressive.

There was a carnival atmosphere outside the ground. It was warm enough for shirtsleeves and the ice cream vans were doing a better trade than the hot dog stands. Everyone was in good spirits: we were going to finish mid-table but, considering we only got promoted the previous year, it had been a good season. There was no roasted chestnut seller so I bought a bag of monkey nuts, instead; Kev bought a 99 and a programme. Next to the turnstile we were queuing at, there was a stocky man selling *National Front News*. Kev got angry and wanted to say something to him but I told him not to because he looked hard and it would only cause trouble.

"But look at him, Billy. He's not much of an advert for the master race. He's a Neanderthal."

"Don't, Kev. He'll hear."

"I don't care. He's an idiot – our two best players are black. We should have a go at people like that. They hate anything different. If they had their way, we wouldn't even be able to walk around dressed like this."

Kev was right, but challenging someone like that would mean exposing yourself and your own views. No one else seemed to be angry about the National Front man and a couple of people even bought his paper. Mostly, though, he was just ignored.

We won the match two-nil, even though we had nothing to play for. Because we had managed to not get relegated, the players started a lap of honour. There was a small pitch invasion and the players had to leave the field; most of the crowd were shouting for the kids to get off. As they were jumping back over the wall on to the terraces, the sight of one of them pulled me up short: the primitive forehead, the malicious expression, the fingers like bananas. It was Bunches, the boy who had threatened to give me a kicking at the youth club in Bromley. I ducked down out of sight and crouched behind Kev.

He twisted round and looked down at me. "What are you doing?"

"It's him. Bunches," I hissed.

Kev surveyed the crowd. "Oh, yeah. And look who he's standing with, now. That NF paper seller. That's no surprise – and they look like each other. He must be Daddy Bunches."

I had no wish to be acquainted with Bunches again, even if we did support the same football team; I dragged Kev away and we left the ground as the players were resuming their parade around the pitch.

I got home from the match before Dad and I went to my room and laid on my bed thinking. How could I be on the same side as Bunches and his dad? Bunches wanted to beat me up for being a punk and his dad hated black people like Dennis White, who was a decent and honourable kid who had spoken out to protect me. Clearly, I was not on the side of Bunches and his dad – we just had a football team in common. We might all watch *Kojak* but that would not make us the same. I was not like them – I was sure of that. But what made one person hate others and another person help others? Was I a hater or a helper? I was probably neither - but I should be a helper. I needed to stop thinking about myself so much and think of others, starting with my family.

"Dad, you know that Deborah has kicked Mole out, don't you?"

"I do. Probably for the best."

He was sitting at the kitchen table reading the Sunday paper in his vest and underpants. It was putting me off my cornflakes. "Are you cooking a roast today?" I asked him.

His eyes did not move from his newspaper. "Yes. I bought a leg of lamb."

"Will there be enough for Deborah and little Michael."

He lowered his newspaper and looked at me. "I should think so. Why?"

"Can we invite them round, then?"

He put his newspaper down. "Ah. I was going to tell you. I've invited someone else round for Sunday dinner."

I knew what was coming. "Who?"

He started to fold his newspaper. "Shirley." The name seemed to stick in his throat and it came out a little strangled.

I feigned ignorance. "Who's Shirley?"

"You know who she is. Shirley Breakspear. Tina's mum."

"Oh. Well, we can all have dinner together, can't we?"

He picked up his newspaper, murmured assent and left the kitchen. I heard the toilet door slam.

In truth, I had some misgivings about us all sitting down to dinner, but I wanted to be some help to Deborah. I had always resented her coming back to live with us time and again but, now Mole had gone and she was in that tower block flat with little Michael, I wanted her to feel as though she was not alone. I walked round to Deborah's and asked her to come to ours later. She looked tired and harassed and seemed grateful to be invited. I forgot to tell her about Shirley.

"Who the bloody hell is Shirley?" Deborah had taken over from Dad in the kitchen and I was helping her with the dinner.

"Has Dad not said anything to you about her? She's his girlfriend, I suppose. She works at the factory. They went away together at Christmas when I was on the school trip. She used to live downstairs. She's Tina's mum."

Deborah pretended to be outraged. "Oh, that Shirley – he's a dirty sod! She's ten years younger than him. Where does she live now?"

"Down in Bromley."

Dad came in and started washing glasses. I could tell he was nervous because he was muttering to himself very quietly. I took the mint sauce into the front room and saw that he had extended the table as though it was Christmas. He had already laid our places and had even put out paper napkins. There was a bottle of wine in the centre; I could not remember us ever having wine. Dad always drank beer and Mum used to have Babycham. The music centre was on and Frank Sinatra was playing. Little Michael was sitting on the floor in front of the telly watching Captain Scarlet. If Dad was aiming for sophistication it was being spoiled by the voice of the Mysterons.

As Dad came in with the clean glasses there was a knock at the front door and he rushed back out again to open it. I heard Dad say Shirley's name and the door close and then there was a hushed conversation between them. Then at normal volume I heard Shirley say, "Oh, Ronnie!" Ronnie? Dad was Ron. Nan and Grandad used to call him Ronald but Mum called him Ron and so did everyone else. No one had ever called him Ronnie.

Ronnie came through the door and vaguely waved his hand in my direction. "You know Billy, don't you?" Shirley smiled at me through her bright red lips and asked me if I was getting on alright at school; I shuffled from foot to foot, nodding. I could see that she was looking me up and down, taking in my paint-spattered trousers and my latest t-shirt, on which I had written X-Ray Spex in pink felt pen. She was dressed in a red tartan skirt and matching waistcoat with a white blouse that had a tumble of frills at her throat; she looked more alarming than I did. I was trying hard not to laugh; I kept expecting her to start Highland dancing like they did on the New Year's Eve telly programme that I used to stay up and watch when I was little. When Dad pointed out little Michael, Shirley went straight over to him and started making a fuss. Deborah came in and Shirley immediately started talking to her warmly about little Michael. Not sure what to do, I went back to the kitchen.

"I didn't know she was in the bloody Bay City Rollers," Deborah laughed, as she came back in the kitchen. "Help me with these plates." She piled the food on and I took them out to the front room one at a time.

When I came back, I said, "She's singing Shang-A-Lang in there," and each time I returned for another plate of food, I said that she had moved on to a different Bay City Rollers hit. By the time I finished with Bye Bye Baby, we were laughing uncontrollably and had to wait in the kitchen to calm down before we went in to eat. Dad called out that our food would be getting cold. He looked at us closely when we sat down because we both looked as though we had been crying.

The talk was stilted as we ate our dinner. Shirley was still milking little Michael as a topic of conversation with Deborah but I could tell she was also prying to find out the details of what had happened between her and Mole. At one point she said, "Oh, it's a shame because I think a little kiddie needs their dad," and I wondered if she was trying to justify the fact that she had buggered off and left Tina with just her dad. I busied myself helping little Michael with his food and Dad was largely silent. He occupied himself with the drinks: me and him had his home brewed beer and Shirley and Deborah were drinking the wine, my sister too enthusiastically, I thought. Shirley kept referring to Dad as Ronnie and, each time she said it, Deborah gave a little smirk; but, as the meal went on, and she had had a few glasses of Blue Nun, she did less to disguise it and the smirk became a grin and then a giggle.

Eventually, Deborah turned to my Dad and said, "So, Ronnie. When are you going to let Billy out again? You can't keep him at home every evening forever."

Dad bristled at her use of Shirley's name for him and mumbled something about having to talk to me about that later. Then Shirley made the mistake of chipping in. "Your dad's very worried about Billy. It's all this punk rock business. He shouldn't be running around with all sorts looking like that."

Deborah turned on her. "I don't know what the bloody hell it's got do with you," she slurred.

Dad looked hurt more than angry. "He lied to me about where he was going. I can't have that."

"Of course he lied – you wouldn't have let him go. Look, he'll be leaving school this time next year. He'll be able to do what he wants. He's found something he wants to do now, something that gets him out of the flat more often and you put a stop to it. Why don't you give him some independence? You did this with me and look what happened. I wasn't used to the freedom and, as soon as I started work, I went wild. Billy has hardly been anywhere since Mum passed. Just locked himself away in his room. A child needs a mum. Dads are more dispensable. You can get by without a dad but not a mum. Everyone needs a mum. I wasn't a child when we lost Mum but Billy was. He doesn't even know how much he's been affected."

Had I been affected? I had thought of Mum dying as just something that had happened, an event in the past that had to be left in the past and we all carried on with the new arrangement. We were

58

a family that did not talk about things like this and Deborah's outburst had stunned me and Dad into silence. I knew that she was not talking just about me: she was reassuring us, and herself, that little Michael would be alright; and she was obviously criticising Shirley as a mother.

It was Shirley who spoke first when Deborah had finished. "There's a big difference between a parent dying and a marriage breaking up, you know. But you're right, Deborah. Your brother has been affected by the loss of his mum. Your dad has struggled on over the last few years but Billy's at a difficult age, now. And that's why I'm going to be moving in to help Ronnie do his best by him."

After all the initial shouting had died down, and they had settled instead into bad-tempered bickering, I had taken little Michael to my room to leave them to it. I had not expected Deborah to so vociferously be my champion but I thought the wine and her emotional state in the wake of kicking Mole out had contributed to that. I was equally surprised at Shirley's bid to be my stand-in mum, although one of the first things I thought of when she said she was moving in was what Tina had said about us all living together. Tina had only been joking but what she had said had alarmed me at the time; now it was going to become a reality, it seemed like a disaster. How was Shirley going to help my dad with me? He always made sure I did my homework and, even though his cooking was not fantastic, we never went hungry. It was true that we just existed side by side; our only common ground was football, and even that had changed as I got older and we went to matches separately. Perhaps that was what Shirley had in mind - she was going to bring us together: family days out followed by us all watching *The Generation Game* on the settee on Saturday evenings. The thought made me shudder.

I heard Shirley getting ready to leave. She was talking to my dad in the hall before she went, telling him it was still the right thing to do. I could tell from their tones of voice that he was feeling miserable but Shirley was putting on a brave face. "It'll all be for the best, Ronnie," I heard her say as she left.

Shortly after, there was a knock at my door. I asked who it was and, when Deborah answered, told her to come in. She opened the door and came and sat down next to me on my bed. She was much calmer. "That bloody tartan terror, eh Billy, what's she like?"

"I don't want her to come and live here."

"I know. I agree. But I can't stop her. I sort of put my foot in it going on about everyone needing a mum and Dad's certain it's the right thing. He said he felt desperate because he doesn't know what to do about you and a woman's touch will make this more of a home for you both, whatever a woman's touch is. But he did say he would feel happier about letting you go out again if things were more stable here, so some good might come of it."

Little Michael was making a picture of me with my felt pens. He had given me trousers and a t-shirt with scribble all over them and really spiky hair. He had drawn my face with a downturned mouth. Deborah gave me a hug and kissed me on the cheek for a second time and told me to come around and see her and little Michael soon.

Dad kept away from me for the rest of the afternoon. At one point I went to the kitchen to get a drink and I could hear that he was watching *The Big Match* in the front room. I went back to my room and did something I realised I had not done for a couple of months: I played some of my Bowie LPs. I started with *The Man Who Sold The World* because a lot of the songs were loud and rocky and then I moved on to *Ziggy Stardust* and *Space Oddity*. I finished with *Hunky Dory* because the songs Changes and Oh! You Pretty Things seemed to sum up my current situation: I had to face the fact that things were going to be different and I was clearly a worry for my dad. I was comforted by the wisdom of the lyrics. I had been neglecting David Bowie; I would not make that mistake again.

In the early evening Dad knocked on my door and said my name; I did not answer. After a while he opened the door and I pretended I was asleep. There was a long pause during which he was not moving but I could hear his breathing. Then the door closed and when I opened my eyes he had gone.

JUNE

I was sprawled backwards over the counter and I could hear the tinkle of perfume bottles as they fell to the tiled floor. The lights above were blinding and the man attacking me was a dark whirling blur. I had my forearms up above my face and his punches were pummelling into them; now and then he landed a blow to my side. I was kicking out wildly with my legs and I knew that sometimes I hurt him because I heard him expel a soft grunt. I could hear Kev shouting somewhere to my left and knew from his words that the other man was assaulting him. One of the women in white dresses with heavily made-up faces was behind me shrieking, "Leave him alone!" over and over again. When the attack abruptly stopped, I slid forward off the counter and slumped to the floor. Two men wearing suits were wrestling with my assailant and he was jabbing his finger at me and screaming something about insulting the Queen. He broke free and ran out of the department store into the street, followed by the man who had been beating up Kev.

The shop assistant who had been trying to help knelt down next to me. "Are you alright, dear? Bloody football hooligans."

One of the men in suits came over and said, "Don't worry, son. The police are on their way."

I looked across at Kev. He seemed to be alright but I could read in his face that he thought we should leave before the coppers arrived. There were make-up samples and perfume testers all over the floor. Some of the bottles had smashed and I could hear the crunch of broken glass as the store detectives tried to move on the shoppers who were gawping at the scene. While the staff were busy picking up the debris, we took our chance; we slipped into the crowd unnoticed and then made our way into the busy throng of Oxford Street outside.

It was the Whitsun half-term holiday and me and Kev had been out all day on a Red Bus Rover. We had been all over the place: up to Ladbroke Grove to a couple of record shops that my boss, John, had told me about; to the Sex Pistols' manager's shop in the Kings Road, although we were too intimidated to go in; finally, we had come to Oxford Street to the 100 Club, where all the groups had performed at a punk festival the year before, but there was nothing to see – just a doorway. It was while we were walking down Oxford Street that two men coming towards us had started shouting and swearing. They were drunk and one of them was wearing a big Union Jack flag like a cape. The England versus Scotland Home International was the next day at Wembley and we had seen supporters of both teams wandering about all day, especially Scotland fans. These two had accents but they were not Scottish; they must have been England supporters from up north. We tried to ignore them and walk past but they turned around and followed; it was us they were shouting and swearing at. We ran into a department store but as soon as we got inside they had caught up and started laying into us.

When it was all over, and we had got clear of the shop, we ducked down a side street and sat down on the pavement behind a phone box. Neither of us was badly hurt: no blood, but we would have some bruises in time. We were not surprised it had happened. Since the Sex Pistols' new single, God Save The Queen, had come out there had been uproar. Dad's newspaper said the song called the Queen a moron and it was especially insulting because it would soon be the Silver Jubilee to celebrate her twenty-five years on the throne. The record had been banned from the radio and Dad and Shirley had both told me to turn it off when they had heard me playing the record at home. They were angry about the cover because the name of the song and the group took the place of the Queen's eyes and mouth. I thought it was the best song I had ever heard: when Johnny Rotten was repeating 'no future', I knew he was talking about me. And it was not just me: the previous Saturday when I was at work, lots of people had come in to buy it: boys from school and kids I recognised from the estate.

Deborah had been right. Since Shirley had moved in, I had been allowed to go out at night again. I had stayed late at Kev's a couple of times and Dad had given me permission to finish our day out by going to the punk club again in the evening, providing Gary was with us. I had the distinct feeling, from the first few weeks of Shirley living with us, that she was not actually that interested in helping

Dad with me. She mostly ignored me and spent large amounts of her time making herself comfortable on the settee watching the telly, listening to her Elvis Presley records or talking on the telephone to her sister. We had never had a telephone before – Dad said they were a waste of money and we could use the phone box or a neighbour's if we needed to – but Shirley had insisted he apply to get one as soon as she knew she was going to move in. She had brought a lot of stuff with her and there were boxes of it everywhere; she had loads of dolls of Spanish flamenco dancers which I found embarrassing and slightly disturbing. It was true that we were eating better since she had arrived but that was the only time we came together; I was spending even more time in my room and I had a sense that the pair of them liked it that way.

We were supposed to meet Gary at Charing Cross Station in the early evening; he was getting the train in from where he worked in Croydon. We had a long time to wait so we went to the Wimpy Bar on Oxford Street and then wandered down Charing Cross Road, stopping at the music shops and admiring the guitars in the window. Kev said he wanted to get one but these were too expensive; he had seen a second hand one in the music shop in the high street and was hoping to get it for his birthday. At the guitar shop near Cambridge Circus, a punk was already looking in the window as we walked up. He was older than us and had perfect peroxide spiky hair. He turned and looked at us. "Alright?" he grinned. "You better watch it, boys. There's a lot of trouble about. Football fans and Teddy Boys everywhere. Heavy night for punk rockers."

We nodded and I told him what had happened to us in Oxford Street, earlier. He said we would be better off getting home as it would only get worse later. Kev said we were going to see the group 999 but we were meeting his big brother first, so we should be okay. He told us to have a good time but to be careful and stalked off up the road as we went in the opposite direction. It was only then that I realised how often we had heard the two-note sound of police sirens; together with the heat of the evening, it made for a feverish atmosphere. Trafalgar Square was full of Scotland supporters and there were police vans parked across the end of the street as we walked across the Strand.

We waited outside the station as Gary had told us to but, twenty minutes after the agreed time, he had still not arrived. Kev started to worry and suggested we go into the station in case he was inside. As we emerged on to the concourse from the ticket hall, the first thing we saw was a crowd of men drinking outside the rail bar. They had greasy quiffs and were wearing brightly coloured drape jackets and brothel creepers: Teddy Boys. Most of them were quite old but a few looked younger. We stopped as soon as we saw them but it was not soon enough. A few looked over and one of them shouted out. We turned and ran. Back out of the station and across the forecourt. I could hear them running after us. Kev turned right, so I went left, hoping they would follow me; they did. I ran down the side of the station, not stopping to look behind; I knew I just had to keep running.

When I reached the river, I halted. I was not being chased anymore - there was no sign of the Teddy Boys. I hoped Kev was safe. I could not go back to Charing Cross to search for him or to find Gary. Teddy Boys carried knives and knuckledusters; I could be in for some real aggro if I fell into their hands. Part of me thought I should just get the bus home but, instead, I decided to walk downriver to Waterloo Bridge and try and find the punk club from that direction. Hopefully, Kev would head there, too; and if Gary turned up, he would go straight there if we were not at the station to meet him.

Being a punk was getting serious; it felt as though we had committed treason. I never knew that people could get so angry on behalf of someone they had never met. I did not really care about the Queen either way, and I was sure she felt the same about people like me. There had been a lot of excitement about the Silver Jubilee on our estate – there was going to be a big party outside with food and music – but I had thought it was about fun rather than making sure everyone had the same opinion. I knew that Dad thought the Queen was 'a wonderful woman' but I remember Mum watching her on the telly and saying she would like to see how she got on carrying heavy shopping back from the market.

When I eventually found the club, there was a queue outside but there was no sign of Kev or Gary. As I walked along the line to the end, a hand shot out and pulled me in; it was Mags. "Billy! Where have you been? The others went in ages ago but I said I'd wait out here in case you came. I'd nearly given up. We thought the Teds had got you."

"They'd have to catch me first," I smiled.

Mags laughed and grabbed my hands. She spun me round and round and started chanting, "Go, Billy, go," over and over. I was bashing into other people in the queue but nobody seemed to care. None of us cared.

On the day of the Jubilee there was no school, so I woke up late. I could sense that things were unfamiliar. Outside my window, I could hear a flock of birds flapping around the courtyard and excited raised voices. When I got out of bed, my room felt different, too. The chair behind the door that I put my clothes on overnight had gone and my trousers were on the floor. I opened my bedroom door and saw that the front door was wide open. Had we been broken into? I called out Dad's name but there was no answer. I went into the kitchen: the table and chairs were not there and, when I went into the front room, the folding table and two chairs were also missing and the music centre had gone. I knocked on Dad's bedroom door but it was silent.

I went out of the front door and looked over the landing wall into the courtyard. There were no birds; the sound I had heard was strings of red, white and blue bunting fluttering in the breeze. They were tied to the landing below us and stretched across the courtyard to the lampposts on the far side. The courtyard was full of people, tables and chairs; they were trying to arrange them in a long line down the middle. I could see my dad; he was wearing a plastic Union Jack bowler hat and looked the most cheerful I had ever seen him. Shirley was there, too; she was wearing a matching skirt and waistcoat like her tartan one, except this had a Union Jack pattern and looked as though it had been knitted. Where did she get such hideous clothes from? I could see Tina's dad and watched for a while to see if him and Shirley were speaking. For the few minutes I observed them, they never so much as gave each other a glance.

They were setting up the kids' tea party for the afternoon and, as I was still technically a child, Dad had been paying money in each week for me to go. I would get to sit with the little kids and have sandwiches, cake, jelly, ice cream, lemonade and be given a commemorative plate at the end. Tina would be there, so I knew I would not be the only teenager. Shirley had been hinting that I should moderate my dress and wear something more 'respectful' for the occasion. That, of course, had made me go the other way; I had spent the previous evening with Kev and Tina customising our clothes. We had each chosen words from the Sex Pistol's God Save The Queen: across the chest of one of dad's old white bri-nylon shirts, I had written NO FUTURE in red and black block capitals; Kev had painted FASCIST REGIME in white on the front of a black t-shirt; in neat print, Tina had put GOD SAVE THE QUEEN itself on her halter neck top. Kev said that was defeating the object as it could be misunderstood as a patriotic statement; but Tina said that was the beauty of it. Kev narrowed his eyes and tilted his head to one side but said nothing further.

Tina had asked what it was like for me living with her mum. I said it was strange because I was used to it only being me and Dad most of the time. She said she was seeing more of her mum than she did before now that she was living upstairs. I could not tell whether she thought it was good, or not. She was a bit more serious than when we had spoken before about my dad's relationship with her mum. I had asked Tina what her dad thought about it all; she said nothing but pulled a startled face, instead.

While I was standing eating my cornflakes, Dad came in through the front door. He went straight into his bedroom and emerged a few minutes later. He had changed his shirt and was wearing a t-shirt that said 'ER 1977' and had a crown and some leaves on it. I had never seen him wearing a t-shirt before. He asked me if I was coming down to help and I said I would as soon as I had got out of my pyjamas and into something more respectful. I was lying; I went back to bed and read. My English teacher had given me a book called *The Loneliness of the Long-Distance Runner* about a boy who is sent to borstal and takes up cross-country. I thought Miss Kelly was giving it to me because she knew I went to athletics club; but she said it was written by one of the angry young men and I would enjoy it. I supposed that, because I was a punk, she must have thought I was an angry young man, too.

In the early afternoon, Deborah arrived. There was no street party for their block – she said every day was a party on that estate – so little Michael was coming to ours. Deborah asked me why I had NO FUTURE written on my shirt and I said that was how I felt: there was not much to look forward to. And I said that the Jubilee felt as though it was about the past; all the flags and bunting were like something from the war. She said that the squatters on her estate had been painting STUFF THE JUBILEE on the walls. She surprised me by saying she agreed with them because it was a waste of money; but I was reminded that she had been a squatter once, too. I felt bad that, just because Deborah was a mum with a child, I had assumed she would not have strong opinions anymore.

We went down into the courtyard. Kids had started sitting down at the long line of tables and people were bringing food out of the ground floor flats. Lots of the small children were dressed up: some were wearing red, white and blue, a few had homemade crowns on their heads and others had hats the same as Dad's. I found Tina and we sat either side of little Michael. The adults were serving the food; Shirley handed us a plate of sandwiches and complimented Tina on her top. She looked puzzled when we both burst out laughing and Tina looked at me as if to say, "See?", and I realised that she had been right. We knew what it meant but the grown-ups were not in on the joke. The sandwiches were fish paste, and even little Michael chose not to eat them; the chipolata sausages were better and we stuffed our faces with those and handfuls of crisps. There were platefuls of specially made Jubilee biscuits with little iced crowns on them, but there was a bit of a fight over the slices of Angel and Battenberg cake; I felt like a little kid. Tina's dad was taking pictures and we posed with our thumbs up; I must have stuck out like a sore one with my spiky hair and NO FUTURE shirt, tucking into jelly and ice cream with all the little ones.

Dad's music centre had been set up outside on a pasting table with a power cable going into Tina's flat because it could not reach ours. He was putting on songs like Sugar, Sugar and Chirpy Chirpy Cheep Cheep. He must have been playing the very records that me

67

and Deborah danced to in the front room on Friday evenings with Mum when we were allowed to stay up later than usual. I had no idea we still had them because I had not seen them for years. Dad had a crowd of kids in front of him, all dancing along; he was in his element. He put on In the Summertime by Mungo Jerry and I saw Deborah looking over at me. We went and joined in, holding one of little Michael's hands each, and danced like we used to.

One of the mums had organised all the seats into two long back-to-back lines for a game of musical chairs. The children started off at a very slow pace and the smallest ones were soon out of the game, including little Michael. But as the number of chairs lessened, the competition got fiercer and fiercer until it was a group of mainly junior school boys shoving each other out of the way, diving for seats and arguing about who got there first. Dad thought this was hilarious and kept stopping the music after only very short bursts, which only increased the tension; but the game had to be abandoned when the remaining three boys crashed onto the concrete fighting over the last two chairs, and one of them cut his knees and his chin.

Tina said she was going to see Kev so I went along with her to see what the party was like at his block. We passed two other parties on our way through the estate. Someone on a balcony shouted "wanker!" at me, and a kid who went to my school called out, "Get some new trousers!" I was wearing my black carpenter's jeans which had almost fallen apart with wear; apart from school trousers, I had hardly worn anything else for months. When we got to Kev's the street party had either finished or not even started. There was a line of tables and chairs but there was no food, no music and no games. There were small children running around but no sign of any grown-ups, except for Gary, who was sitting in a deckchair with his shirt off drinking a can of beer. He stood up and patted me on the back. "Here he is – Billy Whizz. Saved my little brother the other night, Tina. Let a mob of Teds chase him so Kev could get away. Mind you, if my train hadn't been cancelled I'd have got stuck into those greasy toe rags."

"Where is everyone, Gary?" Tina asked.

"They've all pissed off down the pub and left me in charge."

"Is that wise?" I said with mock concern.

"Probably not," he chuckled.

Tina looked around. "Where's Kev?"

"Up there. Can't you hear?"

We listened and could just make out the sound of God Save The Queen coming from their flat. Tina made her way up there and I sat down on another deckchair next to Gary. He gave me one of his beers and we watched the little kids play. I could just make out Johnny Rotten's voice. "God Save The Queen," I said, and clunked my can against Gary's. He repeated my toast and we sat, with the warm sun on our faces, laughing and drinking to the Queen.

When evening came, I walked back to my block with Kev and Tina. Gary said he was going to find Mags. "She's living on your sister's estate now," he told me. When we arrived, Deborah was sitting with some of the grown-ups, drinking; she said she had put little Michael to bed in her old room. There were only some of the older kids still out and the atmosphere had changed: the innocent mood of the daytime had gone and it had become a party for adults. Quite a few of them seemed drunk and were singing along to Elvis Presley; Shirley was dancing with some other women and she looked unsteady on her feet; Dad was laughing loudly with some of his mates from the pub. I walked past him but he did not look my way.

We went up to my bedroom and played records as it seemed we were not welcome outside. We listened to the Ramones and The Clash and David Bowie and then Kev and Tina started kissing so I had to busy myself reading the lyrics to the *Ziggy Stardust* LP. I put on God Save The Queen and Kev started moving my speakers on to the windowsill, facing the window. "Start it again," he said when he had finished. As I put the needle back to the beginning, he threw the windows open wide and turned the volume right up. It was deafening. We could just about hear people outside shouting. We crouched down on the floor, giggling; none of us dared look out. When my bedroom door flew open, I was expecting it to be Dad; but it was Shirley. Her face was shiny and her eyes looked wild. Her lipstick was smudged.

"What the fucking hell do you think you're playing at?" she snarled. Me and Kev looked at her open mouthed but Tina had her head down in embarrassment. Shirley went across to my record player and turned it off without lifting the arm first. It ground to a halt. She spun around and put her face close to mine. "I don't ever want to hear that disgusting shit again," she hissed. "Now have some fucking respect." With that she staggered out of the room, slamming the door behind her.

Tina was sobbing quietly. "That's what she's like. I bloody hate her, I really do." She got up and said she was going home; Kev followed. I wished I was still sitting in the sun drinking with Gary. I went to check that little Michael was still asleep and then, not wanting to risk playing any more records, I laid on my bed reading. *The Loneliness of the Long-Distance Runner* turned out be just one tale in a book of short stories, so I finished it quite quickly. The narrator, Smith, ended up refusing to win a big race to get back at the governor of the borstal. He was winning, but stopped short of the finishing line and let all the others run past him. It made me laugh: what a way to show them that no one could tell him what to do.

When I came out of my bedroom, the flat was in darkness. I could still hear music outside; it was Jim Reeves. I went into the kitchen to get a drink of water and a biscuit. I could hear shouts coming up from the courtyard, at first only one or two, but then more voices joined in. There was an argument going on. I opened the front door and went out onto the landing and looked down. There was a tight knot of about a dozen people next to where Dad's music centre was set up; it seemed to shrink and grow in size and, as it pulsed, it would surge quickly in one direction and then back again. At first, I thought they were dancing the hokey cokey but then I realised it was a fight. There were two men at the centre of it and the others seemed to be either egging them on or trying to stop them, I could not tell which. In the gloomy courtyard lighting, I could just make out that the two men were my dad and Tina's dad. I could hear Deborah's voice continually shouting "Dad!", and then Shirley's voice cut above it barking at them, alternatively, "Ronnie!" and "Ken!" When the knot abruptly came loose, the combatants were exposed and I saw my dad throw two punches and Tina's dad fall to the floor. The knot reformed but this time as two separate units: Dad, upright, was surrounded by his pub mates, and Shirley seemed to be hanging from

70

his neck; Tina's dad, prone, disappeared from view under a crowd of concern and I saw Tina and Kev at the centre.

"Bloody hell!" Deborah appeared at the end of the landing. "Can you believe it? Grown men fighting over what records to play, and whose record player it is, and whose electricity it is. I'm going home."

"What, now?" I said.

"Yes, now," and she went and woke up little Michael.

I said I would walk them home, although what I might do if we met any trouble I was not sure. I was good at running away but that would be difficult with a four-year-old. As we came out of the stairwell, we walked past Dad and Shirley. They saw us go, but we both ignored them; only little Michael called out, "Grandad!" as we passed. There were drunk people everywhere on the walk to Deborah's but, unlike where we had come from, they were mostly good-spirited. Little Michael was tired and we had to take turns carrying him. When we got to Deborah's block, it was all quiet outside; if there was a party going on, it was happening elsewhere on the estate.

The streets were still thronging on my way back again and, despite the warmth of the night and the cheerful mood, I took no chances by keeping my head down and walking quickly with my jacket pulled tightly around me. As I passed one of the pubs, a conga dance came out of the doors; as it snaked alongside, the leader made a grab for me and I only just managed to avoid joining in. The next time I passed a pub, I walked in the middle of the road just in case.

When I got back to the estate, the courtyard was deserted; the fight had obviously killed off the party mood and everyone had gone home. The tables and chairs were still out, but they had been stacked up under the cover of the landings against the walls of the ground floor flats. There had obviously been a clear up because there was a mountain of rubbish sacks at the foot of the stairwell. Dad's music centre was still out on the trestle table but the power cable to Tina's flat was gone. I could not leave it out all night – it would either get ruined or stolen - so I unplugged the speakers and took those up to our flat and left them outside the front door. I made two more trips to get the music centre and the case of records.

As I was getting the equipment inside, I heard a commotion coming from the front room. Voices were raised and I thought there was another argument or fight going on. Dad's voice was loud but he seemed to be forming no words – just snorting and grunting. The only other voice was Shirley's, but it sounded different: there was none of the aggression and hardness I had heard earlier in the evening – it was softer and high-pitched and she seemed to be pleading, repeating Dad's name. He's beating her up, I thought.

When I slowly pushed open the front room door, I knew I could not have been more wrong. They were both on the floor: Shirley underneath with her head thrown back and her Union Jack skirt up around her waist; Dad on top, with a pair of Union Jack underpants around his knees and his white bottom rising and falling. All I could think was, if my English teacher could see this – which in itself was a strange thought to come into my head – she would say, "What is this a metaphor for?" Although I had literally caught my Dad with his pants down, I knew that the scene I was looking at was about much more than just him and Shirley. I closed the door without disturbing them and went to bed.

JULY

Since the Jubilee, and the furore over the Sex Pistols, there were signs at school that me and Kev were not the only kids into punk. I spotted the odd spiky haircut here and there and, one day when I had taken my Clash LP in for no other reason than to walk around with it on show, a few boys I barely knew had made positive passing comments. There were only a couple of weeks of the Fourth Year left and I felt a tremendous sense of relief that the long summer holiday was coming up; but I also had a feeling of dread because the next year was the Fifth Year and O Levels. However, I had been told that, in quite a few of my subjects, I would be taking the easier but worthless CSEs instead, so my expectations had been lowered for me.

At athletics club, we were preparing for sports day. My 1500 metre time had improved but I was not in with a chance of a place: there were boys who were better at the distance than me. The weather was hot, but not like the previous year when the summer went on forever and we had to collect our water from pipes in the street; but training was still hard work and made any sustained effort draining. The middle-distance runners were taking a break and we were watching the sprinters. In front of us, Dennis White was warming up to run the 400 metres. Cummings and Phillips were sprawled out on the grass behind me. They were laughing and I thought it was probably at me, as usual; but then I heard Phillips say, "You know, he's only fast because his ancestors were used to running after their dinner with a spear," and I knew he was talking about Dennis.

Cummings warmed to the theme. "Yes, but you'd think with evolution they'd be getting slower now they can just go to the supermarket. I'm sure you can get goat at Safeway."

"No, they still need to be able to run fast so they can get away from the police when they've mugged little old ladies."

It was not just their prejudice that made me angry, it was their cowardice; I knew they would not dare say that to Dennis's face or speak like that in front of any other black kids. And, after Dennis had intervened on my behalf in the changing room, I felt an obligation to stick up for him. I turned around and looked at them both; I could feel my heart beating really fast. "Why don't you two tossers shut up?"

It came out louder than I had expected and, as soon as I had spoken, I saw McNally get up from where he had been sitting unseen a few yards behind. He came towards us but Cummings and Phillips could not see him. After the look of shock had faded from Phillips' face, he threw his head back and laughed, "Oh! Don't tell me you're a nigger lover, Monson."

"Of course he is; the jungle bunny's his protector," Cummings added.

When McNally barked their names, they visibly jumped and the colour drained from their faces.

"Come with me, now!"

They got up and trotted after him as McNally stomped towards the changing room. Even though he was shouting, it was hard to hear what he was saying from outside. A kid came out and said that McNally was really giving it to them and that he was going to kick them out of athletics club. When I was back out on the track, I saw Cummings and Phillips had changed out of their kit and were leaving the rec.

I was glad that I had challenged Cummings and Phillips and I was delighted they would not be at athletics club any longer; I was feeling quite pleased with myself as I walked to Deborah's to have my tea. I went to either hers or Kev's sometimes after school to keep out of the way of Shirley. I had stopped taking the longer route to Deborah's flat; I had not become braver, it was more that the atmosphere on her estate had changed and walking through it seemed to pose less of a threat. Perhaps it was because of the summer evenings and the fact that it was still daylight whenever I went there; or it could have been that the people were changing. The council were not using the estate to house families anymore, and those already there were gradually being moved away; Deborah had been told that she might be rehoused soon to a more suitable estate. The result of this was that there were less kids about and a lot of the empty flats were being squatted. From my experience of squatters when me and Mum were trying to find Deborah, they were mostly hippy-types like Mole; but the ones on Deborah's estate were different. Once, when I had gone to her flat after school, she was having a cup of tea with a man and a woman of about her age. They were talking about the estate and, although they spoke in quite a posh way, they were a bit too scruffy to be from the council. When they had gone, she said they were squatters from downstairs. Seeing my surprise, she said they were not like the people she squatted with; her new neighbours were more interested in politics than drugs and music.

When I got near to Deborah's block, Mags was walking towards me; she was carrying a full black bin bag in each hand. When she saw me, she ran at me shouting, "Billy Whizz!" She seemed very excited and she hugged me tightly; she smelled of her leather jacket, perfume and cigarettes, and I felt as though I could have stayed there forever.

"I'm moving again," she said, "It's alright here – best squat I've lived in – but it's too far from college. So, I'm going back across the river."

"Do you want any help with your stuff?" I offered.

She looked down at her two bags. "Thanks, but I think I can manage these myself," she laughed.

"What about your other stuff?"

"What other stuff? I don't have any other stuff, Billy. I'm going on the bus right now. Say hello to Gary when you see him."

"Won't you be seeing him?"

She shook her head. "No. I won't be seeing him."

"Aren't you girlfriend and boyfriend anymore?"

"We never really were, Billy. Gary's fun and we've had a great laugh together but he's too much of a normal. He always wants to look after me and it's not what I want. He wanted us to get a flat in Croydon and me to be the little lady. I'd die in a place like Croydon. He wanted us to be like his mum and dad. Your sister's more his type. I've got to go."

She gave me another hug, picked up her bags and then walked away; she turned around and shouted back at me. "Keep going to see groups and I might bump into you. You've got to see The Slits – they're all women!"

Mags was only four years older than me and she gave me hope that I could be as confident as her when I reached nineteen. It seemed unlikely but, if I was, I could ask her out. The age difference would not be as important then. We could live in a squat and I would never ask her to go and live in Croydon; we would go and see punk groups and be right down at the front of the stage together, falling into the equipment; we would talk about how brilliant it was afterwards and she would wrap me in her arms and I would breath in her scent of leather and perfume and cigarettes, and life would be perfect. I waved at her weakly as she hurried off through the estate; I will probably never see you again, I thought.

Deborah wanted to know the latest about the evil Shirley: I could only report that she moved from the factory to the settee to the pub on most days, with the occasional diversion into the kitchen to feed the three of us. All of this, she carried off in an increasingly bizarre range of outfits. I told Deborah that the current favourite was a shiny lime green two-piece – they were always twinsets – with white piping that made her look like something out of the Quality Street tin. There had been no repeat of the aggression she showed on the day of the Jubilee and, thankfully, I had not had the misfortune to walk in on them going at it on the carpet, again. Being reminded of what I had told her about seeing one Union Jack flying high and the other at half-mast, Deborah started making retching noises and jabbing two fingers towards her throat. "Stop it, Billy. It's just too horrible."

I asked Deborah if she had seen Mole. Not only had he not been to see little Michael, he had given her no money for weeks and she had no idea where he was. Since he went, she had stopped the few hours of work at the pub that she had been doing, as it was too difficult with little Michael. Although she got social security and child benefit, it was not enough and money was tight. She said she would not accept any financial help from Dad but she would be alright; the tin of beans that she shared out three ways on toast was a contradiction. In any case, she said, she was already looking for a job for September, when little Michael would be starting school. I felt guilty for not offering to look after him when Mole had gone, so she could go to work; I also made a note not to stay for tea the next time I visited – I felt as though I was taking food from their mouths.

I took little Michael down to the play area to give Deborah a break. We had it all to ourselves; he loved being pushed on the swings and went down the slide countless times and never got bored. When we went back upstairs, we watched *Rentaghost* on the telly, which I thought was hilarious but little Michael hardly laughed. I noticed the Ramones LP was propped up on the floor by the record player. I supposed it could have been Mole's but, as I was leaving, I said, "I didn't have you down as a Ramones fan, Deborah."

"Oh, it's not mine. Somebody left it here. It's Gary's, actually." She coloured a little as she spoke and looked away. I had taken Mags's comment about my sister being more Gary's type as just an example, but I now saw that there was a basis for what she had said. They had never been great friends but they were the same age and were sometimes part of the same crowd; and Gary had been comforting Deborah at her party. I wondered if he had an ulterior motive when he told her what Mole was up to. Not that I disapproved: Gary was one of the kindest and most reliable people I knew - if he was part of our family, he would more than compensate for the presence of Shirley Twinset.

The next day at school, I had to go with McNally to see old Burkett. I frantically tried to flatten my hair down as we waited outside before the secretary said we could go in. Having never seen the inside of the headmaster's office for the first three years at school, it was the second time I had been there in a few months. Burkett looked like he was from another time: he had slicked down oily grey hair and a heavily lined pale face. There was a plume of smoke rising from a cigarette balanced on the ashtray next to him on the desk. The smoke engulfed him and his whole appearance was completely colourless, someone who existed only in black and white. I had never seen him wear it, but I noticed that hanging on the back of the door was a black gown and hat like the teachers wore in

77

Winker Watson in *The Dandy*. I had to tell old Burkett what Cummings and Phillips had said about Dennis White and what I had said to them. I included 'tosser', and thought I might get in trouble for that. McNally then repeated what they had said to me within his earshot and old Burkett asked me if I agreed that was what they said; I did. The headmaster thanked me for answering his questions and said I could leave; he said nothing about my hair or my use of the word 'tosser'. When I closed the door, I saw Caroline and Peter, Cummings' mum and dad, sitting in the secretary's office with another couple.

At break, I found Kev and told him what had happened at athletics club and how I had been to the Headmaster's office. He said it was good that McNally was taking it seriously; other teachers would dismiss it as mickey taking and not do anything about it. He said there were too many people in the school being racialist and he was surprised that boys like Cummings and Phillips would talk like that. I knew exactly what he meant: they were in the upper stream, like Kev, and he thought they should not be prejudiced. Bigotry was alright for stupid kids but the intelligent should know better. I had heard my dad make derogatory comments about black people and he would certainly have been in the lower stream at school; what I wanted to say was that I was not like Cummings and Phillips but I knew it was wrong to judge and abuse people because of the colour of their skin. Kev said that the National Front were planning to hold a march from near the local college down to the high street in a few weeks' time and the police had refused to ban it; he said there would be a big demonstration to try and stop it and we should go along to show whose side we were on.

After school I waited for Kev outside the gates so we could walk back to his place. While I was waiting, Cummings and Phillips walked past; they saw me and laughed, as they always did, but there seemed to be a more malicious tone than usual. When Kev came out, he looked annoyed. "Have you heard that those two tossers have got away with it?"

"What, Cummings and Phillips?"

"Yeah. They were just boasting about it in Chemistry. McNally wanted them punished and kicked out of athletics club but Burkett

78

gave in because their parents came in and they've got away with a detention with Simmons, who is going to educate them about racial discrimination. They were laughing about it. I can't believe it - it's a joke."

So, this was what happened when you stood up to people. Nothing. And they would be back at athletics club as normal. I wondered what to do: perhaps I should give up running; or I could tell Dennis White what they had said about him. He would do something. It had been hard enough challenging Cummings and Philips in the first place and now I would have to repeat their insults to Dennis; but that would be the right thing to do. "Don't worry," I said to Kev, "I'm going to do something about it."

At athletics club, Cummings and Phillips swanned into the changing room as if they had grown a few inches since the last training session. Most of the kids knew that there had been some sort of altercation between me and them and there had been mutterings amongst the black boys about exactly what it had been about. I had only told Kev what had been said and I was sure he had not been spreading it around; but Cummings and Phillips could not help shouting their mouths off no matter what the consequences for them would be.

Dennis was already out on the rec and I went over to talk to him but, before I could say anything, McNally called us both over. I thought he was going to say something about the incident but instead he started to outline what he wanted us to do on the track. We started with a 400 metres that only the two of us ran. McNally told Dennis to run slightly behind his usual pace so that I could keep up with him all the way around. It was hard work, but I managed to stay level with Dennis for the distance. While Dennis was resting, McNally started another 400 metres with the others, but included me as well. He told me I had to come in the first four but I only managed fifth because I had had no rest. We repeated this – a race with only me and Dennis, followed by a race with the other 400 metre runners and me – three times. I kept pace with Dennis each time and, after two attempts, managed to finish fourth in the larger field, and then third. I was shattered by the end of it and, as I lay on the grass, Dennis sat down next to me. "What was that all about?" he said, gesturing at the track with his forefinger.

"I'm not sure," I panted. "I think he might be putting me in for the 400 but, without rest, I did worse than I usually would. I didn't see the point."

"Nah, me neither."

"Listen, Dennis. I need to tell you something."

"If it's about those two stuck-up kids, save your breath, Billy. I know, already."

I was about to ask him what he was going to do about it when McNally came over and sat down with us. "I'm entering both of you for the 800 metres on sports day, as well as your usual distances."

"Why?" said Dennis and, when it was explained to us, we both knew that McNally was already doing something about Cummings and Phillips.

The morning of sports day, the air outside was still and thick; I could tell it was going to be stiflingly hot. As I walked to school, the sun was already high and hot and the weeds in the pavement cracks were wilting and parched. It was not going to be the best conditions for running one middle-distance race, let alone two. I was nervous about both races: I wanted to do well in the 1500 but I had to save some energy for the 800, which came soon after. The only consolation was that there were junior and intermediate races at each distance so there would be some rest time between my two senior events. I had asked Dad if he could come and watch but he said work would not give him the time off. However, Deborah said she would be bringing little Michael to cheer me on.

I only had the first two lessons and then I had to go to the gym with all the other competitors so that we could then walk to the rec with the PE teachers. In English, Miss Kelly asked me if I had enjoyed *The Loneliness of the Long-Distance Runner*. I said I had but I was surprised by the ending. She asked me if I had any plans to do something similar at sports day. I laughed and said I should be so lucky to be so far ahead. She smiled and gave me a knowing look.

The gym was full of noise. The First Years were particularly excited, as it was their first sports day. It was mine, too, as a competitor; I had only ever been a spectator before. I had been a good runner at primary school but at secondary school I had made no effort in PE, until now, and I found it hard to recall why. I went and sat with the other Fourth Years; Dennis looked deadly serious when he nodded at me, which encouraged and pressured me at the same time. I could see Cummings and Philips clowning around; they were laughing and pushing and jostling each other. They looked as though they did not have a care in the world, I was tense and uneasy.

At the rec, the caretakers were setting out chairs by the finish line - these were for teachers and parents – and they had roped-off large areas where all the boys who were not competing would sit on the grass; one along the home straight, another along the back straight near the field events. The whole school came down to watch sports day and it struck me that I would be running in front of five hundred people; the thought only served to increase my anxiety. There was a table on the opposite side of the finish line: there were trophies and medals on it and McNally was sitting at one end, fiddling with the last-lap bell; one of the music teachers, Mr Mitchell, was setting up a microphone and speaker at the other end.

There was not enough room for us all inside, so I got into my kit behind the changing room with a lot of the younger boys. I had no wish to be near Cummings and Phillips, listening to their bragging. They had both been good athletes all the way through school: they always beat older kids and came first and second in the 800 metres – the winner varying - and they both competed in the high jump, as well. I was glad I had no field events to distract me. Dennis was in the triple jump and the long jump, on top of the 400 metres and now the 800; he would be worn out.

As we were taking part, we were allowed to wait under the shade of the trees at the end of the rec until our events were called. Senior teachers and spectators had started to arrive and I could see old Burkett sitting at the front of the seated section with the school governors. Little Michael was on the grass further back and Deborah was sitting on a chair next to him. As the other kids were turning up and being told where to sit by their teachers, a voice came over the speaker and called for competitors for the discus and shot put for each age group. I felt sick: I knew that my first race would begin soon.

It was a shock coming out of the shade into the full sun; I could feel it burning my shoulders as I walked to the start of the 1500 metres. When I passed the kids from school sitting along the home straight, Kev stood up and shouted out, "Go on, Billy!" I turned and looked at him and he did a double thumbs-up and pulled a stupid face. I waved at little Michael but he failed to recognise me. I thought old Burkett was staring at me and, when I looked down, I saw my shadow and my perfectly spiky hair.

At the starting line, the Fifth Years seemed to tower over me. A proper starting pistol was being used, which made me jump when its sharp crack signalled that we had begun. The immediate pace shocked me, as it always did - did they not know we had to go around the track nearly four times before we could stop? – but I tucked myself in somewhere near the middle and tried to keep pace with the kid in front of me. After we had passed the finish line twice, I felt that I could move up and I went past two boys; but on the last lap, the pace increased and the group in front of me pulled away. I finished fourth.

Back in the shade, I heard the results of some of the senior field events being announced: Phillips had come first in the high jump and Cummings second; Dennis had won the long jump. Down at the starting line, the junior 800 metres was about to begin; it would not be long before my second race. Dennis came back from the long jump pit. I gave him my congratulations on winning, which he accepted with a nod. He said he had completed his first triple jump and would probably not have to jump again as it was his personal best and unlikely to be bettered by anyone. He said it in a matter of fact way, without a hint of arrogance; what I would have given for such quiet confidence.

When the call came for senior 800 metres runners to go to the start, I thought I was going to throw up. Dennis asked me if I was alright and I said I would be in a few minutes – when it was all over. We walked quickly to the starting line; we were the first there and took up positions in the inside lane as McNally had told us to. As the others arrived, they were bunched along the line; I could see

Cummings and Phillips at the edge of my vision, higher up the curve. At the sound of the pistol, Dennis was off like a shot at 400 metre-pace, with me following close behind. I could sense that none of the other runners were trying to, or could, keep up with us. As we went down the back straight, some of the watching kids were up on their feet. I could tell that they knew they were witnessing something special. We were running really bloody fast and, as we came out of the bend into the home straight, I could see that the pack were almost 100 metres behind us. Dennis increased the pace and I managed to keep with him. At the finish line and the bell, I went past Dennis, as agreed. I just heard him say, "Go Billy, go," as he fell away, and I tried to keep the same pace. It was killing me; I felt as though my heart would burst through the wall of my chest. As I came into the back straight again, I looked across and saw that Cummings and Phillips had broken from the pack and overtaken Dennis and they were already halfway through the bend. I thought I was going to die. The spectators on the back straight were all on their feet now, shouting indecipherably. It was impossible to keep the pace and I knew that I had slowed down. On the top bend, I looked back and Cummings and Phillips were close behind, running side by side, gaining on me. I took the bend into the home straight too wide and then they were on the inside, level with me. I tried to find something more to sprint for the finish, but I could not pull away from them. I could hear Kev screaming my name over and over above the din of the other kids. To the right, the spectators in the seated area were all on their feet, too, and I could see Miss Kelly jumping up and down. When I looked to my left, Cummings and Phillips were marginally ahead of me; I could see the finish coming up and I searched for one final burst and then I ducked for the tape and sprawled onto the grass behind the line.

I was on my hands and knees, breathless and panting. Someone touched me on the back and then put a small square of card into my hand; I looked up to see it was one of the PE teachers. I opened my hand and looked down at the card; it was blank. I turned it over; written on it in black felt pen was, '1st'. Cummings and Phillips were sitting a little way from me. The PE teacher was handing them pieces of card. They looked at them and then both slumped backwards. I wanted to go over to them and wave my card in their faces; instead, I got up and went to where Dennis was lying, face down on the grass. I shook his shoulder and, when he raised his head, put the card in front of his face. He looked up at me and, for the first time since I had been doing athletics, I saw him smile. I went to the results table and gave the card to McNally. He took it from me without a trace of emotion and simply said, "Well done, Monson." As I turned away, Cummings and Phillips were behind me with their cards; I looked right through them and started to walk back to the shade with Dennis. We passed the seated area and Deborah was there, with a frown on her face and her arms outstretched, palms facing upwards in a gesture of incomprehension. Kev called out asking me who had won and I just smiled at him and kept walking. When we got to the trees, I heard McNally announcing our victory and the deafening cheer that went up immediately after.

AUGUST

Unexpectedly, I now had friends. Vanquishing the smart-arse pair of Cummings and Phillips at sports day, defeating them - as the joke went - by a spiky hair's breadth in front of the whole school, had made me into some sort of luminary. A collection of fellow-traveller proto-punks – boys from our school and girls from Tina's school - had coalesced around me and Kev, and the fact that I worked in the record shop and Kev had a guitar and was starting a group, made us leading lights of this little gang. I thought that one of the girls liked me but I had given up on the idea of a girlfriend: my previous infatuations had only led to a permanent sense of disappointment. We had started hanging around in the high street on Saturday afternoons when I had finished work, looking at the records each other had bought, or in my case, taken in lieu of wages. I had bought an LP by The Damned, a live compilation recorded at the punk club we had been to, and an LP by Iggy Pop, which had David Bowie on it. I was not sure if Iggy Pop was punk, but I liked him because Bowie played on his record. Because there were so few punk LPs, I had started buying singles again, and John gave me the odd one for free. I had bought the Sex Pistols' Pretty Vacant and Sheena Is A Punk Rocker by the Ramones, but it was the singles I had by small groups like The Users, The Cortinas and The Adverts that really excited me. I loved The Adverts' One Chord Wonders: it was unlike anything I had ever heard; the group sounded as if they did not care what people thought of them at all.

We sometimes went to a shop called Panoply, at the far end of the high street. It had always sold hippy clothes, such as afghan coats, cheesecloth shirts and ponchos, but it had started to stock some punk stuff. The clothes were too expensive for us but it sold cheap accessories: we all bought small badges with the names of punk groups on them, and I had got some blue plastic sandals and a pair of white-framed 1950s sunglasses. Although we condemned the holey mohair jumpers and deliberately ripped trousers as being for poseurs, we would hang around in the incense-filled shop and the woman who ran it tolerated us in the hope that we would attract more business. 'Poseur' had become our favourite word to describe people who made a token effort to make their appearance temporarily punky but were not brave enough to commit to something more permanent, like a haircut; we also called them 'plastics'. The irony was that quite a few of our number were certainly poseurs and plastics, but we overlooked this fact.

On the second Saturday of the month, Dad and Shirley Twinset went off on holiday to Camber Sands. Dad had asked me if I wanted to come but I could tell by the way he said it that he would rather I stayed behind. So, I was stopping over at Deborah's for the week and we planned to take little Michael out on some day trips. I finished work at eleven because John was closing the shop early; it was the day of the National Front march and, like some other shopkeepers in the high street, John feared that there would be trouble. Me and Kev were going to the demonstration against the march and then onto football because there was a pre-season friendly match. A couple of our little punk tribe were coming to the protest, too, but most of them were worried that there would be aggro and were keeping out of the way; there had been a National Front march in North London a few months earlier, and fighting had broken out and arrests had been made as people tried to stop the march.

It was a warm but overcast day that started with a rally at the rec. There were vans full of police lined up in the street outside and Kev said that his brother had seen dozens of police vans parked up on waste ground behind the high street. When the whole school had been at the rec on sports day, there was about five hundred people. There were a lot more there for the rally and Kev said there must be about ten times as many. There were placards and banners in the crowd: they read, 'ONE RACE – THE HUMAN RACE' and 'UNITE TO FIGHT RACIALISM'. I took a sticker from a Socialist Worker newspaper seller that said NAZIS OFF THE STREETS and stuck it on my t-shirt next to my football badge and a Sex Pistols badge I was wearing. There was a platform at the front of the crowd; the mayor made a speech through a megaphone. He said that all good people were opposed to the National Front march as it was an attack on our racially mixed community and he blamed the police and government for allowing it to go ahead. Then there were speeches by a bishop and others and it all got a bit repetitive and boring. Then one of the speakers said we were going to march down the high street to show our opposition to the fascists. He said it was important to demonstrate peacefully but some people booed and a chant of 'smash the National Front' went around the crowd.

As we were leaving the rec, I saw Miss Kelly and McNally from school; they were holding hands. Miss Kelly saw me and seemed surprised and excited that me and Kev were there. She said, "Well done, boys," and McNally said we were good lads. It made me feel grown-up that we were involved in something worthwhile but at the same time I felt patronised because they saw it as exceptional that fifteen-year-olds should have a view about something serious. Then I realised that quite a few other teachers from school were nearby; Simmons and Mitchell, the music teacher, were each holding one end of a large red banner that said 'TEACHERS AGAINST FASCISTS'. Even Simmons smiled at me.

Soon after we had left the rec, the march started to split in two. People were peeling away from the route and drifting into a road that went around the back of the high street. They were mostly the younger demonstrators and they started running and urging others to join them. The police tried to stop them but there were too many and they soon gave up. Kev pulled me by the arm. "Come on, let's follow them. They're going to the college to stop the NF."

I looked back at the main body of our march. I could see the teachers' red banner bobbing along above a sea of heads as they moved away from us. There seemed to be as many marchers going in our direction as those still making their way to the high street. Chanting kept breaking out as we walked along; it was like football, except half the crowd were black and the other half were students. Apart from me and Kev and the two from our small social group, I saw no other punks. We wound down a series of back streets until we came out on the main road past the other end of the high street.

As we neared the college, I could see there was already a crowd outside and its size took my breath away: there were as many people as had been at the rec but in a space much smaller. A number of roads met outside the college and, usually, they were choked with traffic; but there were no cars or buses. Instead, they were all packed with people and it looked as though they would not be able to absorb our crowd. People were swaying backwards and forwards and chanting 'the workers united will never be defeated'. I realised that there was a line of police across the top of the road opposite the college and people were pushing against it to try and break through. There were photographers clambering up lampposts for a better vantage point and a television camera crew was filming from the roof of the public toilets. I heard someone call my name and, when I looked around, I could see Dennis and his mates in the crush a few feet away from me. I squeezed my way through and asked him what was happening. He told me the NF were behind the police line waiting to start their march. "But they ain't gonna get through without a fight," he said, and I saw him smile for the second time.

I felt people pushing against me with more force and, when I turned to see the others, they were not there. I thought I could see them further away but I was knocked backwards and lost my balance. It was only the density of the crowd that kept me on my feet. When I had regained my footing, I had lost sight of Kev. The police were pushing into the demonstrators, driving a wedge through the middle, forcing us into two groups; they were trying to open up a path for the National Front march. By turns we were squashed up against each other and then large spaces would open up, momentarily freeing us. I could see the sticks from placards being thrown, flying through the air on to the police. The sun had come out, and I felt hot. The noise was overwhelming and dizzying: sirens, chanting, angry shouts and then the clatter of horses' hooves - mounted police were riding into the crowd. I found myself near to one of the two police lines that was holding back the swarm; I was wedged up against the wall of a pub and, only a few feet from me, demonstrators were fighting the police. I was scared and felt as though I might pass out. Something thrown from behind landed near me and at once the air was full of choking orange smoke; above me, a police horse reared up out of the haze like a phantom as its rider tried to get in between us and his colleagues. I was pushed around the corner of the pub and into the road the police had been protecting. Scores more police arrived and started dragging people away – by their hair, by their feet, by their arms. I was frightened they would arrest me so I tried to keep behind others. Then all movement seemed to stop and the crowd grew quiet; but the lull lasted only seconds and was replaced by a huge roar. I realised that the march had started. It was hard for me to see but I caught sight of hundreds of police helmets, their silver badges glinting in the sunlight, and behind them dozens of Union Jacks on poles. As soon as the crowd could see that the police were bringing the National Front through, flanking them in protection, they started to throw anything to hand: cans, bottles, coins. The houses next to the pub were derelict and people were hurling the debris from the front gardens: bricks, wood, glass, corrugated iron. One man ran right up to the police and launched a dustbin into the march. Police started to neglect their escort duties to tackle the demonstrators, leaving the march unprotected in places. People broke through and started attacking the National Front and grabbing their flags. There was hand-to-hand fighting going on all around me. It was chaos; but even amongst all the disarray, I had time to think that the National Front all looked like my dad. Just as I was trying to push backwards into the crowd to avoid the violence, an NF marcher appeared in front of me, screaming and shouting abuse; it took me a moment to understand that it was me he was abusing. He came right up to me; a vein was pulsing in his right temple and I could smell his bad breath. He started jabbing his finger in my chest and then he screamed in my face, "If I ever see you down at the football you're fucking dead, son!" I looked down and remembered I had my football badge on next to my NAZIS OFF THE STREET sticker. Before I could do anything, someone punched him and he fell to the floor. I turned and got away; as I did, it dawned on me that the man was the NF newspaper seller, Bunches' dad.

I was surprised at how quickly the crowd around me started to thin out, once the march had set off. I could hear the commotion receding into the distance as the National Front passed more demonstrators up ahead. I stayed where I was; the street was littered with broken bricks and glass and discarded placards and Union Jacks. A procession of Black Marias pulled up and the police that were holding demonstrators began to load them into the vans; I started moving in case I got swept up in the arrests. I could have walked to football from there but I was unnerved by Bunches' dad's threat. He did not know who I was - he had simply been enraged by the sight of my badge next to an anti-NF sticker and he was unlikely to be at the pre-season friendly - but if he looked out for me and found me at a future match, there would be some aggro. However, I was sickened by his assumption that, because I went to football, I should support the National Front. I could not stay away because of an idiot like him, so I started heading to the ground.

Out on the main road by the college, I saw Kev; he was standing at a bus stop looking lost. He looked relieved when he saw me. "What happened to you?"

"I've had a scary bloody time," I told him. "What about you?"

"It was crazy. I thought I was going to get nicked. I hadn't done anything but a copper grabbed me. Then a load of other people pulled him off me and I got away."

I told Kev what had happened to me - the smoke bomb, the police horses, the bricks, Bunches' dad - and he said he wished he had got that close to the NF. I said we should get a move on if we were going to football but Kev said we should give it a miss as this was much more exciting; we should follow the march to see what else was going to happen. I had forgotten that the original demonstration would still be in the high street and the National Front march was heading that way; the police would have to keep the two groups apart again.

As we walked down the hill away from the college and towards the high street, we came across straggling groups of demonstrators and saw evidence that there had been missiles and violence aimed at the National Front all the way along. Rocks and sticks were scattered across the road and, every so often, we saw police leading arrested people off to vans. We started to jog to catch up with the NF march but there was no sign of it. The debris in the road lessened and we reached a small group of demonstrators facing a line of police blocking off one of the side streets. As we carried on, there were police across every turning; we knew that they had taken the NF away from the high street and they were not going to let demonstrators anywhere near them.

90

In the high street, all the shops were closed and many had their shutters down. The market had packed up early and the traffic had stopped; there were hundreds of waiting demonstrators. The police were trying to move them on but they were angry that the National Front were being protected; those that argued were getting arrested. Scuffles with the police were breaking out everywhere and I said to Kev that we should move away; I had no wish to get so close to the action again. We jumped over a traffic barrier and went and stood with a group of onlookers outside the department store, opposite the clock tower.

More police arrived and charged at the crowd to get them to move but they only ran a little way and then stopped and turned and started to throw things. Soon, the police were facing a barrage of rocks; it was like watching Northern Ireland on the news. The police charged again and arrested a few demonstrators but most of them regrouped a little further on and continued with their hail of stones; I saw some police being carried away with head injuries. A squad car came speeding out of their ranks and drove towards the demonstrators. People fled but others pelted the car and it quickly reversed back. Some shop windows got smashed and I could see that something was on fire further up the high street. I had never seen so many police in one place but they had lost control; kids were running out of the smashed shops with stuff in their hands and no one stopped them. This is a riot, I thought; this is anarchy - and in my high street.

Kev heard it first: above the noise of the tumult and the turmoil, a drumming sound. We did not know where it was coming from but it was gradually increasing in volume. When its source appeared from around the corner, it was a shock. Rows of police beating their truncheons against head-to-floor see-through shields, were advancing slowly up the high street like a Roman legion. Missiles crashed into the shields but they had no effect - the police kept on coming. Banks of Black Marias were rolling along ominously behind the lines and, further back, more police started arresting anyone on the street, even if they were just watching. Kev must have been reading my mind: "Looks like the fun's over. I think it's time to go home, Billy."

For the next few days, the news reported Saturday's events as a riot and a battle. Some of the reports said that trouble had been stirred up by outside political agitators but me and Kev and Dennis had been there and we were local; and our teachers, too. Deborah had bought a newspaper and they seemed to be obsessed with numbers: 5,000 police, 4,000 demonstrators, 500 National Front marchers, 200 arrests, 100 injured demonstrators, 50 injured police. It was the smallest number that preoccupied them most; the front page had a photograph of a policeman with the headline, WHO WILL DEFEND HIM? A lot of people had got hurt and I had found it a terrifying experience but at the same time it was exciting; and I felt proud that we had stood up for our area. The mayor had asked the government and the police to ban the National Front march because it would cause trouble; they had not listened and the mayor had been exactly right and now everyone was horrified. It made me think adults were a bit stupid; all that trouble so a load of fat, middle-aged racialists could march about with their flags.

Early on Tuesday morning, there was still a TV camera crew in the high street when we were walking to the train station. I was going on a day out to Hastings with Deborah and little Michael; we had chosen Hastings because Mum had taken us there a couple of times in the summer holidays when we were younger. Gary had taken the day off work and was coming too, which made it clear to me that he had become close to my sister. At the last minute, Kev and Tina had decided to come, as well; I was unsure if my sister was happy with our swollen party but if she resented it, it did not show. At the station, the platform for trains into the centre of London was crowded but we stood on the opposite one on our own. The people across from us were miserable; it was already a hot day and they looked sweaty and flustered, crammed against each other waiting for their train. It made me think, even more, that having a job was grim.

When our train pulled in, it was virtually empty. The hot air inside hit us like a wall and we pushed all the windows down and sat on the sun-scorched cushioned seats in high spirits as we rattled off towards the coast. Gradually the buildings thinned out and within half an hour we were in open green countryside. We had to get off at Sevenoaks and wait for another train which, when it arrived, was packed with groups of people like us, talking too loudly. We carried on through the countryside and, every so often, little Michael would look out of the window at the horizon and ask if it was the sea. I recognised some of the station names, particularly Battle because Mum had told me that was where the Battle of Hastings had really taken place; when I was little, I thought it was a bit too much of a coincidence that a battle had happened at a place called Battle. But the main reason I remembered Battle was because, once we had passed it, I knew we were nearly at the seaside.

We walked in a day-tripper procession along the curving street that led away from the station and down to the town. Some families had come well-prepared, laden down with buckets and spades, rubber rings, folding chairs and picnic baskets. We were an odd bunch: we had hardly anything with us and we were an unlikely alliance between a young couple in their early twenties with their kid – or so it seemed - and a trio of teenage punk rockers. Tina had put green and blue food dye in her hair and, although it had faded, it still turned heads. Me and Kev had both sewn zips into our trousers, like The Clash, and Kev had made a WHITE RIOT t-shirt. I was wearing my sunglasses and plastic sandals and a t-shirt that I had cut holes in and drawn on in red felt pen to make it look like I had bullet wounds.

Deborah and Gary took little Michael on the miniature railway that ran along the seafront while the rest of us went to one of the big amusement arcades. Dad had given me a few quid to spend while he was away but I wanted to hold on to as much of it as I could. I had a go on a pinball machine but I thought it was a waste so I switched to Waterfall because you could win quite easily by knocking coins off of each of the ledges until they fell into the tray; I did win some money but I put in more than I got back. I tried the one-armed bandits and the fruit machines for a while but I was not sure what to do when you were asked to hold or nudge. Kev and Tina were playing Pong and were shrieking with laughter; lights were flashing on the machines and their ringing and trilling was giving me a headache. We had come to the coast for sun and sea and we were spending our time in the gloom of an arcade; I went and waited outside.

When we had all met up again, we caught the lift that was like a train carriage that went straight up the side of the cliff to the top of the hills above the town. There was an old castle there and I took little Michael to climb over the ruins. We played King of the Castle and he never tired of pushing me off of walls and stones. We sat on a ledge up above an archway and looked out to sea; the sun was at its highest and it reflected on the water like broken glass. Deborah and Gary and Kev and Tina sat on the grass below us; their contentment in their coupled states made me feel excluded. Gary went to an ice cream van and came back with 99s for us all so we clambered down and joined them.

We got the lift back down and went and sat on the beach. Deborah bought little Michael a bucket and spade but he could only collect shells and pebbles in it on the stony beach. Gary suggested going to the pub but Deborah said we had better get something proper to eat first, so we wandered to the end of the beach where the tall black sheds that the fishermen kept their nets in were. There were a couple of fish 'n' chip restaurants and we went in the less crowded one and had cod and chips, buttered bread and tea. We started talking about the riot and Deborah said I should not let Dad know how close to all the trouble I had been. Kev had an argument with his brother because Gary said that we should leave it to the blacks to fight the National Front. Kev got angry and said we all had a duty to fight fascism and got even angrier when Gary laughed at him and said he sounded like a student.

Afterwards, Gary went into the pub and came out with some bottles of beer and Kev bought a plastic football from one of the gift shops. We went and sat back on the beach and I took little Michael down to the water's edge and took his shoes and socks off so he could have a paddle. I rolled up my trousers but kept my plastic sandals on. Kev and Gary started an energetic game of heading tennis. I had to keep wading in to the sea to retrieve the ball because Gary was so useless. "You must have a pointed head," Kev said to him.

The fourth time I had to do it, I realised my left plastic sandal had come off. I held my bare foot up for the others to see. "I've lost my sandal."

94

Everyone laughed, except Deborah who said, "Don't worry, it should get washed back up soon."

I carried on paddling with little Michael but kept looking out for my sandal. The longer it went on without reappearing the more the others kept laughing at me, even Deborah. Gary and Kev went and sat back down. I led little Michael back over to Deborah so she could dry his feet; it was hard to walk on the pebbles with my bare foot and it really hurt.

I went back down to the shoreline and waited; another ten minutes went by but there was no sign of my sandal. "Oh, this is bloody ridiculous!" I shouted, and I could hear a howl of laughter from behind me. Kev came and stood with me, as if to offer moral support; but I could tell he was choking back tears of laughter. I was so annoyed that I pulled off my right sandal and threw that into the sea, as well. Almost straight away, it got washed back up. Kev snatched it out of the foam. "Why don't you keep it, Billy, just in case the other one does turn up?"

"No. It won't. Throw it back."

Kev looked at the sandal. "Hold on a minute. This is your left sandal, the first one you lost. You've just thrown your other one in for no reason." He turned and held it up to the others. "His sandal's come back!" he shouted, "but he's thrown his other one in!"

Deborah and Tina were doubled over with laughter and Gary was laying on his back, kicking his legs in the air and bellowing. I grabbed the sandal from Kev. "Oh, just piss off and leave me alone," I told him. Deborah had said my sandal would come back and it had; the other one would come back, too – I would just have to wait. I sat down at the water's edge and stared straight ahead.

I waited for an hour but the sea stubbornly refused to surrender my right sandal. During that time, Deborah came down and sat next to me. "Come on. Forget about it. We're going to play crazy golf." She was trying to commiserate but she was grinning. "Try and see the funny side."

Eventually, I gave up and limped along the beach to the crazy golf course wearing my one sandal; I was greeted with gales of laughter. Gary went off to the gift shop and came back with a pair of flip flops for me. I put them on to cheers and I could not help but smile.

We stopped at a pub for a drink on the way back to the railway station; we sat outside and everyone kept deliberately treading on my toes under the table. Little Michael fell asleep and Gary had to carry him the rest of the way. On the train on the way home, Tina said she had felt so happy being with us all in the sun by the sea; she said she wished the summer holidays would never end and she wanted to stay fifteen forever. Deborah gave her a cuddle and I could see my sister had tears in her eyes.

The next day, I went home in the afternoon to pick up my baseball boots. Flip flops had been alright in Hastings but, as soon as we had got back to London, I felt an idiot walking in them. When I looked up at our flat from the courtyard, I could see the curtains were drawn – I was sure I had left them open. Outside the front door, I thought I could hear music playing; when I went in, it was confirmed - there was music coming from the front room. I opened the door but the room was dark; apart from the music, there were other noises coming from the settee. As my eyes grew accustomed to the gloom, I realised it was Shirley Twinset. She was cuddling a cushion and sobbing uncontrollably; her face was tear-stained with mascara. My first thought was something had happened to Dad; but then he appeared behind me.

"What's going on, Dad? I thought you were on holiday."

"We've had to come home early. Shirley's too upset."

"Why? What's happened?"

"Haven't you heard? Elvis is dead."

SEPTEMBER

The death of Elvis cast a long shadow over the rest of the summer; Shirley Twinset was inconsolable and stayed off work for another week after the holiday at Camber Sands had been ruined. She never left the flat and the sound of Elvis drifted into every room, night and day, until I could sense even Dad was getting fed up with it; he would have been different if it was Sinatra. Shirley's self-confinement had ended in spectacular fashion: in her bereavement, she had been obsessed with some Elvis records that her ex-husband had kept when they split up. She kept asking Dad to go down and get them but he was reluctant. After his fight with Tina's dad on Silver Jubilee night, I sensed he was embarrassed by his behaviour and in no rush to renew the conflict. Eventually one night, having wound herself up with so much Campari and *King Creole*, Shirley went storming down to the landing below and started hammering on the front door. I listened at a window and could hear her shouting, "Give me my Elvis records, you bastard!" What Tina's dad was saying I could not hear but when Shirley started screeching, "What are you fucking doing?!" I ran out to see what was happening. She was down in the courtyard picking up LPs and every few seconds another one would come frisbeeing out into the warm night air from the landing below; I could hear Tina's dad laughing. When Shirley came back to the flat, sobbing and clutching a ragged pile of records - some with ripped covers - to her chest, she went straight into the front room where Dad was pretending nothing had been happening and I heard her scream at him, "Are you going to let him get away with that?!" Dad's complete silence on the matter was an answer in the affirmative that Shirley Twinset was not expecting. It occurred to me that it was the loss of her marriage that was upsetting her as much as the loss of Elvis. The next day she went back to the factory and her records featured less and less on the front room music centre in the evenings.

The weekend before school started again, I met Deborah and little Michael after I had finished work. He was starting in the infants that week and was very excited. We were taking him to buy a school satchel; he did not really need one, but he had it in his head from something he had seen on *Play School* that he did. We went to a small shop at the end of the high street that had its windows lined with yellow transparent plastic film and sold boots, shoes and bags; I had never noticed it before. We were served by a very polite old man who wore a shopkeeper's coat like Ronnie Barker did in *Open All Hours*. Little Michael chose a brown leather satchel which cost a lot less than Deborah thought it would; I paid a pound towards it. The strap was too long for little Michael, so the man made some extra holes in it with a tool that looked like a pointed screwdriver. When we left, he said, "Good day to you." We thanked him and outside we both said at the same time, "What a nice man," and laughed at the coincidence. I though how much our relationship had changed for the better this year.

"I'm getting a job there." Deborah was pointing at a shop off the high street that said Community Law Centre above it.

Deborah had said she was looking for a job for when little Michael started school. "How did you get it?" I asked.

"That couple who were at my flat when you came around – the squatters from downstairs – they work there. They're solicitors. They told me about the job."

"Did you have an interview?" The thought of a job interview terrified me.

"I did but it was very short. They just wanted to know a bit about me and if I had any experience. It's just basic office stuff – answering the 'phone, typing, filing. It's only for four hours a day while Michael's at school but it's a start. I did work in an office once, you know."

"I know, I remember. It was for two weeks, wasn't it?"

"Yeah, alright, I know; but I hated it there. They were so stuck-up. This is a really good place; they help people who need advice but can't afford to go to a firm of solicitors. They helped me sort out my social security when I kicked Mole out."

I was glad for Deborah. I worried about her less now that Gary was on the scene, but it was still a comfort that she would not be stuck in that flat on her own all day.

As we approached Deborah's tower block, she stopped dead in her tracks. Mole's van was in one of the parking spaces. "Oh, shit," she said and then stopped herself from saying anymore for little Michaels's benefit.

He had seen it, too, though. "Dad!" he shouted and ran into the lobby and kept pressing the lift button.

In the flat, Mole was out on the balcony, smoking and drinking tea. He looked just the same as when I had last seen him. He came in and made a fuss of his son and little Michael was clearly delighted to see him. I had not even thought about how little Michael might have felt when his dad had gone; he saw only his dad, not the scruffy tosser that I saw. A big Tonka Toys tipper truck was on the settee and little Michael ripped it out of its cardboard box when Mole gave it to him. We pushed it across the front room carpet to each other while Deborah and Mole went in to the kitchen. I could hear them talking; at first it seemed calm enough but, after a few minutes, there was the occasional rise in volume of both voices. Deborah had not seen him for three months and he had given her no money to help with little Michael in that time. The talking stopped and Mole came out and gave me a cup of tea. "I can see you're right into punk rock now, man." He still called me man. "I like your strides. They're solid, man." Solid?

"Yeah, right." I was a little embarrassed because I was wearing a pair of black PVC trousers that I had bought from a mail order ad in the back of the NME; on the two previous occasions I had worn them – once at work, once when I had gone to Kev's – people had made comments. They stood out much more than all my other trousers and left no doubt about my punk rocker status.

Mole turned to Michael. "Right, come on little man. We're going down to the playground, me and you." He leapt up and ran to the door and I could hear him chatting away to his dad as they went out. I went out on the balcony and looked down, waiting for them to emerge from the entrance. Michael appeared first, running. Then Mole, with his usual shuffling gait; even from a bird's eye view, I could see the regular puffs of smoke dancing around his head. I watched him pushing little Michael on the swings, going down the slide with him, chasing him around the roundabout. I thought that I should make more of an effort with Mole, like I had with Deborah. He was Michael's dad; he might not be living with him but he was part of our family.

Deborah appeared behind me. "Well, that was a surprise," she said. "We haven't seen him for three months and then he turns up out of the blue as though it was only yesterday." I asked her where he had been and she said he had been working up north. He was squatting again now, in Camberwell, but not working. "Hardly any money to give me, as usual, and he wastes it on that." She pointed at the tipper truck; it was the biggest Tonka Toy Michael had ever had and must have cost a few bob.

When they returned to the flat, Deborah made us all cheese on toast. Mole told little Michael he would be back next weekend to take him out to the pictures. Deborah looked annoyed and I wondered if she would prefer it if he was not around at all. Perhaps she thought her relationship with Gary would be complicated if Mole started making regular visits. He said he had better be going and Deborah asked if he had forgotten something; he fished around in his pockets before handing over a few pound notes and a door key. She sighed when he had gone and said, "This is all I need."

"He is his dad," I ventured, but Deborah was staring into space and said nothing in reply.

Kev was a picture of concentration; brow furrowed, tongue sticking out of the corner of his mouth, he was sitting on his bed hunched over the fretboard of his electric guitar. Despite its distorted buzz coming from the small practice amp on the floor, Tina's singing could be heard loudly and clearly above it. We were attempting to get all the way through the Ramones' Blitzkrieg Bop without making a mistake, and I was playing the drums - although I did not have actual drums. Instead, we had salvaged two large cardboard boxes from around the back of Safeway's and I was hitting them with a pair of Kev's mum's knitting needles. She had already been in twice; not

100

to ask for her needles back but, firstly, to ask us if we could keep the row down and, secondly, if we wanted a sausage sandwich each.

Kev had worked out how to play the guitar to three other songs, as well: two were also from the Ramones LP – Judy Is A Punk and Let's Dance – and the other was You Really Got Me by The Kinks which, although it was really old, sounded like a punk song. His dad had showed him how to play something called barre chords, where Kev put his index finger across all of the strings and formed his other three fingers into a kind of claw; he then had to hold that shape and simply move it up and down the fretboard to change chord. Kev's dad said it was like driving an automatic car instead of a manual. We had also written a song ourselves, called Lewisham; I was quietly amazed that we had composed something. I had done most of the words and Kev had come up with the music; I thought it was the song we played best and it was better than covering other groups' tunes. However, the most positive part of our bedroom practising had been Tina's voice. She was embarrassed to sing in front of us at first, and would turn her back, but after a while she lost her inhibitions. Her voice was quite high but very strong and had a strange sort of warble at the end of some of the words. I was the most disappointing of our trio; I struggled to keep time and it made my arms ache, even though the songs were all short.

When we stopped, Kev got on to a familiar theme. "We need to get some proper equipment – drums and a microphone. We can't get anywhere like this. And we need a bass player." We had been practising for the past few weeks and, every time we met, Kev made the same desperate statement. Neither of us disagreed with him but we had no money to do anything about it; and even I knew we needed more than Kev thought we did; microphones had to be plugged into something and his guitar needed more than an amp the size of a shoebox. As for a bass player, we had no idea where to find one of those; none of our little tribe of high street punks seemed able or willing to fill the gap in our group, so we had resorted to placing an advert in the window of the record shop. John had offered to display it for free; it said, BASSIST WANTED – APPLY WITHIN. I thought we should be more specific and mention punk but Kev said being open-minded was important.

We might have been incomplete when it came to personnel but we already had our poses for the covers of *Sounds* and *NME* clear in our minds and what the sleeve of our debut single would look like. Most importantly, we had a name for our group. It had not been easy, though. Agreement had been difficult and we had been known by a dozen names in two weeks, some of them for less than an hour. We had been The Mysterons, Helicopter Crash, Daktari, Johnny and the Animals, The Useless, The Bored, Rebel Rebel, Mine All Mine, Hooligan Outlaw, Phloem and the Xylems, The Things and The Cranks. We were currently The Un-Named; it was rather uninspiring but it had stuck for three days, which was a record. I preferred Phloem and the Xylems, because it had an X in it, but I was not going to reopen the debate now.

I had an idea. "We could talk to Mr Mitchell to see if we can use some of the music equipment at school. We might be able to practise there." But I immediately saw the flaw in my own plan. "Tina wouldn't be able to, though."

"No," Tina said, "but it's worth asking. You might be able to play some real drums and Kev could use a proper amp. I can just practise singing here with Kev and his guitar."

Kev agreed. "And we could ask Mitchell if he knows any kids at school who play the bass. Not one single person has answered the advert."

We played Blitzkrieg Bop one more time and then Kev's mum came in and said we had to stop because they were having trouble hearing Dave Allen on the telly.

Dennis and his friends all congregated at the top of the playground near the tuck shop. I was nervous approaching them. They were laughing at the little First Years trying to keep their places in the queue in the daily scrum to get served. I had not been to the tuck shop at break time for years because it was a free for all. It puzzled me why the teachers were never there to supervise. When I had been a First Year, I had never managed to get served before the bell went at the end of break. Once, I had actually got to the front of the queue but there was such a crush of kids behind me that my arms became trapped and, although I managed to get my hand in my pocket, I could not get the coins out to pay for the Wagon Wheel I had asked for. The dinner lady kept barking at me with my Wagon Wheel in one of her giant hands and the other held open for the money; but I could not raise my arm up to the counter. The bell had gone and the hatch slammed shut in my face, with me unfulfilled yet again. It was my last visit to the tuck shop.

His mates were all so tall that I had to weave through a forest of them to find Dennis. He was leaning against the fence at the back and nodded when he saw me. "I need to talk to you," I said and he followed me further down the fence away from his crowd.

"You gotta be kidding me. Me in a punk rock group? That's a laugh. Have you noticed that I'm black? Punk's for white kids like you. I'm into reggae music, yeah?" Dennis had considered my invitation for him to join Dead Future - we had changed our name yet again – for a few seconds before rejecting it. Mitchell had told us that Dennis's brother, Trevor, who had left school two years earlier, was a bassist. He suggested asking Dennis if he played. He did – sort of.

I tried to convince him that we had something in common. "Punk's like reggae – it's not music for normal people. We're all outsiders. We both get trouble because of what we look like."

"Are you trying to tell me that getting picked on for being a punk is the same sort of thing as I get for being black from the NF and all the other racialists around here?" He shook his head and I realised I had sounded stupid.

"No, I'm not. What I really mean is that both types of music are against oppression - it's all rebel music."

Dennis sighed. "You're talking a lot of shit, Billy."

"I know." It was my turn to sigh. "But we don't know anyone else."

He laughed. "I'll practise with you a little bit to help you out. I'm not that good yet, you know - I'm still learning - but I've got my brother's old bass and an amp and speaker."

"Nice one. Mitchell says we can practise in one of the music rooms after school on Monday. Just bring your bass because we can use the school's amps. See you." I ran off to tell Kev that we had a bass player.

The front page of the evening paper stopped me outside the newsagents. There was a picture that showed a car. I could just about tell it was a Mini. It was twisted and smashed into a zigzag shape from the front all the way to the rear seats. Part of the number plate could still be seen; it read FOX 66. The headline above the photograph said MARC BOLAN KILLED and above that, in smaller letters, 'Pop star's car smashes into tree.' On the right was a picture of Marc singing into a microphone, his corkscrew hair illuminated white. At the very top of the newspaper front page was a small photograph of his girlfriend, Gloria Jones, who was still alive. It was years since I had liked T Rex but I was shocked by the news. I had only seen Marc Bolan on the telly two days before; he was trying to revitalise his career with a show called, *Marc*, and a couple of punk groups - The Jam and The Boomtown Rats - had been guests on the programme. Pop stars were supposed to inhabit another world yet, exactly a month after Elvis had died of a heart attack on the toilet, another one had died in a car crash. They seemed deaths too ordinary; drug overdoses and plane crashes would have been more glamorous. Marc Bolan was the first person whose picture I had put up on my bedroom wall. I had them everywhere at one time. I felt overwhelmed.

I was on my way home from school but, instead, I went into the shop and bought the newspaper and then went around to Deborah's flat. I showed her the front page but she already knew. She looked at me closely for a long time and then asked, with surprise in her voice, if I was alright. I found it difficult to answer as, each time I went to speak, I felt tears welling up inside of me. When she asked if I was upset, I started sobbing. She put her arm around me and sat me down on a kitchen chair and made a fuss of me. "What is it, Billy? What's wrong? Why are you so upset about Marc Bolan?"

I had no idea why it had affected me so much. I thought about Shirley and the state she had been in over Elvis. I had thought at the time that perhaps she was actually distressed about something else - was I upset about something else? "I don't know," I said.

"Billy, you didn't even get like this when Mum died." As soon as she had spoken, I could see that she regretted saying it; but it was too late. At the mention of Mum, my sobbing turned to weeping and then to wailing; and, to my embarrassment, I could not stop.

Playing a real drum kit was very different from two cardboard boxes. It was like patting your head and rubbing your stomach at the same time. I had a foot pedal for the bass drum and one for the hi-hat cymbal and I had to coordinate my feet and arms. It was hard. Mitchell tried to show me a basic rhythm using the snare drum and the hi-hat but I found it easier to use the tom toms and the bass drum most of the time. It was exhausting. Dennis said that me and him had to make sure we were working together but I kept getting ahead of him. Dennis complained that we were playing too fast but Kev said he was playing too slow. Dennis just smiled and said it was the roots rock reggae rhythm. His bass sounded amazing and it made the floor of the music room vibrate but the songs were so different – every one of them sounded like The Clash's Police & Thieves. Kev enjoyed himself, though; his guitar was loud and beefy, not like the waspish whine of his practice amp, and he did Tina's vocals, as well. How he could easily do the two things at once, when I was having such trouble with my own dexterity, annoyed me. Dennis picked up the songs quickly and, gradually, our differences in pace found a compromise. Mitchell stuck his head in and said it sounded interesting but he wanted to go home so we would have to leave. I had to lug the drumkit back to the outside store cupboard at the top of the playground, next to the tuck shop. I cursed being the drummer; it was hard work on two counts.

Dennis lived near Kev and when we got to his block, he asked me if I had five minutes because he wanted me to listen to some drumming. He said I was too loud and fast and needed to be more relaxed; he had clearly missed the point about punk. I hesitated but said yes; I realised, to my shame, I had never been in a black family's home before. Dennis politely introduced me to his mum and I felt stupid when I responded with a formal, "It's very nice to meet you." She had a regal air about her and I was quite intimidated, but she said I was welcome and asked me if I wanted a cup of tea. We sat in the front room and drank our tea while Dennis's mum asked us questions about school. There was a radiogram, just like one we used to have, behind the door; I was surprised to see a Jim Reeves LP on top of it. Afterwards, we went to Dennis's room, which had two beds in it; he obviously shared with one of his brothers. Between the beds there was an old-fashioned record player with a built-in speaker and a lid that closed like a suitcase. Dennis took an LP from a slim pile under his bed. He put it on and handed me the yellow cover. At first, I thought it was by The Clash, because it had the word CLASH on the front in red but then I realised that, with the two black words in front, it formed the title, TWO SEVENS CLASH. The group was called Culture and there was a picture of them silhouetted against a sun-drenched sea; there was also two large overlapping gold sevens, like a front door number. "Bad things happen when the two sevens clash," Dennis said ominously. "Like the National Front and that." He played the title track and told me to listen to the drums. It had a very simple beat that had lots of echo on it. It sounded like it was only the snare drum and it seemed easy enough; but every now and then there was a fast rat-a-tat-tat around the rest of the drum kit. I told Dennis that bit was too complicated for me; he laughed and said I was probably right. I said I liked the song, though.

Since I had made a fool of myself crying like a baby at Deborah's, she had been treating me as though I was fragile. I still had no real explanation myself why I had been so overcome, but she was convinced that I was experiencing some sort of delayed reaction to mum's death. Perhaps I was, because I had been unaffected by Marc Bolan's death since; his telly programme had carried on being shown - he must have recorded them all in advance - and I had watched it without a glimmer of grief. I had gone to Deborah's after school to watch the last episode of the series. I was excited because David Bowie was going to be on singing his new single "Heroes", which I had already got from the shop, and I was also hoping a punk band might be on. I had not seen Bowie on the telly for a couple of years. There had been an *Omnibus* documentary about him that Dad had let me stay up and watch. Bowie was thin and acted strangely and Dad kept saying he was a freak and a crank. I thought he looked ill and I had worried about him for weeks after.

I had been playing "Heroes" constantly and had fallen in love with it. The lyrics about kissing by the wall were so romantic and made me think of Mags, and even Sophie for the first time in ages, and I thought the idea of being heroes for a day was very punk; I felt that Bowie was connecting with me, somehow. I watched the show with little Michael and we jumped around the front room to Generation X and then Eddie and the Hot Rods. Eventually, Bowie came on and I called Deborah in.

"Bloody hell, he's still good looking," she said. She was right; he was not ill anymore and he was wearing a plain blue shirt and his hair was a bit spiky on top. He was very serious as he sang the song but the music sounded weedy compared to the record, like groups always did on *Top of the Pops*. When he had finished, he played guitar with Marc Bolan; they did an instrumental as the credits rolled and, right at the end, Bolan fell into the microphone stand and Bowie broke into a broad grin. I wondered how he felt now that his friend had died.

Deborah went back into the kitchen to get little Michael's tea. There was a knock at the front door and she called out for me to answer it. "It'll be Mole," she said. When I opened the door, Mole was standing there and so was Gary; he was his usual self but Mole looked awkward and angry. He grunted as he pushed past me. Gary said, "We met in the lift," and winked at me as he came in. The kitchen door was shut so me and Gary went and sat in the front room. I had not seen him since our day out at the seaside and I asked him what he had been up to.

"Oh, you know, this and that. I tell you where I have been going. This place in Croydon where they have punk bands on every Sunday night. Big place. You need to come. There's some right good groups coming up."

"Sunday night. It's a school night. I'm not sure I'd be allowed."

"Come on. Do you want me to have a word with your old man? Everyone's playing. Generation X, Siouxsie and the Banshees, Buzzcocks."

I wanted to see all of those groups. "No, it's alright, thanks. I'll ask him."

"That sounds interesting." Gary jerked his thumb in the direction of the kitchen where we could hear Mole and Deborah's raised voices. Little Michael came into the front room crying. "Alright, mate. What's up?" Gary gave him a cuddle and sat him down on the settee. "You sit here and watch the telly with your uncles. Don't you worry about it."

Mole appeared in the doorway with a wild look on his face. When he saw little Michael squashed between me and Gary, he bit his lip and was about to say something but thought the better of it. He disappeared from view and Gary burst out laughing. We heard Mole shout, "Fuck the lot of you," and the front door slammed.

Deborah came in. "Don't you go winding him up more than he already is. I don't need this."

Gary said, "I didn't say anything to him, Deb - honest," and he winked at me again.

OCTOBER

Gary had not taken Mole's return well; and Mole had responded to Gary's constant presence in a similar way. But in Gary's typically bullish manner, he had started a campaign of letting Mole know just how much at home he was with his ex and his son. If he knew when Mole was visiting, Gary would make sure he turned up, too. Mole had got into the habit of picking little Michael up on Saturday mornings and Gary would always be arriving at the flat to see Deborah just as Mole was leaving. On the occasion I witnessed them arrive together, Deborah had let slip when Mole was coming around to give her some money, and Gary had got off work early and hung around outside until he saw Mole's van swing around the corner. His war of attrition had worked because Mole had failed to appear on the following Saturday to take little Michael out. Deborah was not happy about what Gary was doing: it had caused arguments between her and Mole - sometimes in front of their son - and she did not want him to have an excuse to avoid his responsibilities. However, she liked Gary being around but worried about the effect on little Michael of having both his dad and another father figure in his life.

It was Sunday lunchtime and Deborah had come to see Dad but him and Shirley had already gone to the pub. Little Michael was watching *Joe 90* in the front room and we were drinking tea in the kitchen. "I like Gary - he's reliable, and I know he'd be a better dad to Michael, but I'm not sure I want what he wants."

I was slightly uncomfortable having such a grown-up conversation with my big sister but that was how she treated me now – like an adult. "What does he want?"

"He wants us to go and live in Croydon. But I'd have to give up my job if I did that. And work have said they'll give me day release to go to college after Christmas to do an A Level in Law. I don't want to move – I've moved home so many times. I know the block's a bit shitty but I like the flat – it's big. I shackled myself to Mole when I was sixteen, Billy, not much older than you are now - what an idiot I was. I might have a four-year-old kid but I'm young and I could still do something with my life. I want Gary to accept that. I don't want to drive him away – he's a good man. There are not many like him around. "

I wondered about Gary. He had asked Mags to move to Croydon with him, too. It sounded as though he wanted to settle down with whoever he could get to agree to it. "I thought you might have to move out of the flat soon, anyway. Aren't the council rehousing everyone who has kids from your block?"

"I've heard nothing for months. At work they said the council are having trouble getting people to move to flats with smaller rooms." She took a swig of tea. "Do you like Gary?"

Her direct question wrongfooted me. "Yeah, of course, you know I like Gary. Little Michael likes Gary. Dad likes Gary. Everyone likes Gary."

"Yeah," she said absentmindedly, "everyone likes Gary."

When they had gone home, I laid on my bed reading. I was going to Croydon in the evening to see a group and had nothing to do until then. Miss Kelly had given me another book by the author of *The Loneliness of the Long-Distance Runner*. It was called *Saturday Night and Sunday Morning* and was about a young bloke called Arthur who worked in a factory. He knew that life was rubbish but his answer was to think he was better than everyone else, get drunk all the time and have affairs with the wives of his workmates. He was loud and angry; I was not keen on Arthur. Whatever he thought he was, he was still just working in a factory like they wanted him to.

I had been to Croydon with Gary and Kev and Tina the previous Sunday night to see Generation X. The venue was on the first floor of an office block and was big – much larger than the punk club we had been to in the West End. There were a lot of plastics there: kids who had covered their clothes with safety pins and badges to disguise how straight they really were. We had gone on the bus and it had taken forever; Tina's cousin, Lorraine, had got on when it went through Bromley. She had changed since I had last seen her: her hair was short and spiky on top but long at the back and she had a heavy fringe at the front. She was wearing a leather jacket like the one Mags had and looked quite punky. She asked me how I was getting on with her dreaded Aunty Shirley and I just pulled a face. She said she would never forget when I pogoed at her local youth club and asked if I had been avoiding her because she had been to my local youth club a few times but I was never there. I said not to take it personally but I was not keen on the youth club. The truth was, I had been thinking about going with Kev and Tina because some of our little high street punk gang went, too; but I had always set myself against it and would have felt stupid suddenly changing my mind. However, I was going to have to go soon, anyway, as Kev had arranged for our group to play there in November. I was quite petrified at the thought.

Dad had let me go to Croydon again because Gary had assured him he would look after me and our first trip had been uneventful. Siouxsie and the Banshees were playing; I was looking forward to seeing them because I had never heard them – they were always in the music papers but they had not released any records yet. When we got there, there was a long queue snaking across the front of the building and away down a narrow side street. When we eventually got to the entrance, the sign on the door said that The Slits were the support group. Mags had mentioned The Slits and they had done a session on John Peel a couple of weeks earlier. They had sounded frantic and sang about stealing from shops and obsessive boyfriends. Kev had taped it and we had been listening to it constantly; he wanted us to play one of their songs, called Newtown, but there was a guitar part that he could not work out. When he saw the sign, he said now he would be able to see how they did it.

We went into the big bar area and the first person I saw across the room was Mags. She looked different but it was unmistakably her. Her hair was cropped and dyed peroxide blonde but I recognised her make-up. She was at the centre of a big crowd of punks and was laughing and dancing around. I pointed her out to Gary and he went straight over to her; she screamed when she saw him, leapt on him and wrapped her legs around his waist. She was wearing the same PVC trousers as me. They stayed like that for a couple of minutes, deep in conversation, and then he must have said something about me; she looked in my direction, jumped down and came weaving across the bar shouting, "Billy Whizz!". When she reached me, she

111

hugged me and whispered, "Nice trousers," and rubbed her leg against mine, which nearly made me pass out. Then, laughing, she said loudly, "I'm in Croydon after all."

I asked her if she lived there and she said to not be so stupid – she had only come down to see The Slits. I told her about our group, Panic Stations - we had another new name - and she made a fuss of Tina when I said she was the singer. "Good for you," she kept saying, "good for you." She promised to come and see us play at the youth club. "I wouldn't miss it for the world."

When she had gone back to her mates, I said to Gary how good it was to see Mags. "She seems really happy."

"Happy?" he said. "She's off her bloody nut. I worry about her."

She was at the front of the stage when The Slits were playing, throwing herself about, looking completely at home. The Slits were fantastic – so chaotic and energetic; I wished our group could be more like them. Kev was fed up because the guitarist turned her back to the crowd when she played the part he had struggled to work out. I told him not to worry – he could play anything he wanted to.

We went right down the front to wait for Siouxsie and the Banshees. A man came on stage and said there could be no pogo dancing because the floor may collapse. When the group started playing, the song was slow and dramatic and then it sped up until it was at a frenzied pace; everyone ignored the instruction and we became one jumping, heaving mass. There was a real crush against the stage and Siouxsie told the audience to move back because people were getting squashed; bouncers kept pulling people out of the throng and dragging them across the stage to safety. I was trapped against a monitor and was having trouble holding back the crowd behind me. Eventually, I was pulled out, too, and I spent the rest of the time watching from the side of the stage with other survivors of the swarm.

On the way out, I saw Mags queuing for the toilets; she waved me over. "I will definitely come and see your group. Look, I've written the date on my hand."

"Brilliant. I'll see you then." I went to catch up with the others but turned back to her. "Gary's worried about you, you know."

112

She looked weary. "Oh, tell him to stop. He's not my dad. I'm just having a good time, Billy - the time of my fucking life."

There had been tension at home because there were going to be redundancies at the factory. Some of the biscuit production was being moved up north and one part of the building closed down and sold off. Who would be affected was going to be announced on Friday afternoon. All week Dad and Shirley Twinset had been speculating; he worked in the warehouse and she was on the production line and, by turns, they each claimed they were more or less likely to be made redundant. On Friday morning I could hear them snapping at each other over breakfast so I stayed in bed until they had both gone off to work.

I went to Kev's straight after school and sat in while him and Tina practised The Slits' song we had rehearsed at school with Dennis. We spoke about Dennis: I said it was obvious he did not want to play with us at the youth club; Kev agreed but said what else could we do? He was the only bass player we had and it would be too late to try and find a replacement now. We also had an argument – something me and Kev had hardly ever done. I suggested we do a version of David Bowie's "Heroes" but Kev was immediately resistant. "Why? It's so plodding."

"Yeah," I said, "but we can speed it up, can't we."

"It's probably too complicated to learn."

"Oh, come on. I don't know anything about the guitar but it sounds pretty simple to me. It can't have more than three chords, can it?"

"Maybe, I don't know. But look, Billy, haven't you been paying attention? Heroes? We don't have heroes – No More Heroes, yeah?"

I was getting exasperated. "No, you haven't been listening. The song's about us being heroes, being our own heroes. What could be more punk than that?"

"You're right, I haven't been listening. Why would I want to listen to David Bowie? He's a superstar has-been and I don't know why you bother with him."

By any measure, Kev had gone too far. "Well, if that's how you feel, perhaps we should do the poxy Stranglers' song, then," I shouted.

My raised voice stunned us both into silence. Tina looked shocked but then rescued the situation. "I think this is what they call musical differences."

When I came out of Kev's flat there was a fog that had not been there when we had walked home from school. The temperature had dropped and the air was cold on my face. The streetlights had begun to spark into life and their pale orange glow shone dimly through the vapour. As I walked through the estate, block after block rose up out of the haze and faded as quickly as they had appeared. There was no one about and all sound was muffled by the mist. I felt like I was the last person on earth.

I thought about Mags; I had not even asked her where she was living. I wondered where she was right at that moment and what she was doing. Probably in the West End, off her nut, as Gary would say; or having the time of her fucking life, as she had put it.

The flat was in darkness and I thought that Dad and Shirley must have gone out but I soon realised that the flat was exactly as I had left it in the morning. The breakfast things were still in the sink and the flat felt cold from a day of being unoccupied. I wondered where they were. I played the "Heroes" single again; it was a great song and I would get Bowie's new LP that it came from when I went to work the next day. Releasing two LPs in the same year was unusual but Iggy Pop had just done it and so had his mate; I was still going to bother with Bowie, whatever Kev may say.

I washed up and made some cheese on toast for my tea and started watching a film about Evil Knievel but I quickly got bored. The flat felt less empty with movement and light from the telly so I turned the sound right down instead of switching it off. I read my book: Arthur started going out with a girl called Doreen but then he got badly beaten up by the husband of one of the women he was still having an affair with; he deserved it. I turned the sound back up when the news came on. It was about the Yorkshire Ripper, as usual.

I was just getting ready to go to bed, when I heard voices outside the front door. It was Dad and Shirley. They were talking too loudly and taking ages to come in. There was a thump and Shirley shrieked with laughter; I could hear Dad's voice grumbling. I went and opened the door; Dad was sitting on the floor and Shirley was trying to pull him up. They were both, very obviously, very drunk. They must have gone straight to the pub after work. Dad looked up at me. "Fifteen years, Billy, fifteen years. Can you fucking believe it? The dirty bastards."

I helped Dad up and we got him onto the settee. He just kept repeating the same things over and over again. Shirley was not as drunk and I managed to understand from her that there were going to be fifty redundancies at the factory and both of them were on the list. She then joined in with Dad's woeful wailing, except her mantra was eight years. I went and made them both some coffee, because that was what you were supposed to do, but what I really wanted was to go to bed. They were both losing their jobs; it was a disaster.

"Oh, no! What are they going to do?" Deborah was not entirely surprised at the news. "I'd heard there were going to be redundancies - but both of them? That's bad luck."

"They don't think it's luck. They're convinced Shirley's ex had something to do with it." They had seized upon the fact that he was not being made redundant and was good mates with the foreman. They thought it was Tina's dad's revenge: for Shirley leaving him and for Dad beating him up.

"They'll have to go on the dole until they can get jobs. But they'll be fifty people round here looking for work." Deborah was not making me feel any better about the situation.

"I know. It's not good. And it's happening quickly, too. They finish at the end of this month. I'm worried what it's going to be like at home."

"I hope he doesn't do anything stupid. He was out of work when you were born and Mum told me that he wanted to move us all to Bracknell because there were jobs there - but she put her foot down."

This alarmed me. "Bracknell? Where's that?"

Deborah was not sure. "It's one of those New Towns, somewhere outside of London."

A New Town. Like The Slits song. That would be dreadful. I would rather stay where we were and starve than move somewhere like that.

I asked Deborah if she had made any decision about moving, herself. She said she had and was staying in the flat, for now. She had told Gary that she enjoyed her job and was looking forward to going to college and hoped he could support her in trying to better herself; but she had assured him she liked him being around and he was welcome to move in if he wanted to. But she had made it clear that he had to respect that Mole was little Michael's dad and would be visiting sometimes. "Mind you, Mole's disappeared again," she sighed.

"How did Gary take it? Is he happy to settle for moving in to your flat?" Mags had been right: it was obvious he wanted nothing more than to replicate the happy home life of his own parents.

"He's alright. You know Gary. He said he would do whatever I wanted and he can't wait to move in. But he's ever hopeful. When I finished my big speech he said, "So we still might move to Croydon one day?""

I had started working in the record shop all day on Saturday so I had not been going to football. Despite being threatened by Bunches' dad at the NF march, I had still gone to a couple of matches at the start of the season; I had even seen him selling his newspaper but he had not recognised me. Our encounter was probably just one of a number he had on a day of violent confrontations; I had told myself there was no reason why he should remember me. As a result, I was not scared of going to games but, when John offered me some extra hours, I said yes. Football had been getting less and less important to me and I needed the money; it was an easy decision to make.

The last Saturday of the month was going to be an important day: *Never Mind the Bollocks, Here's the Sex Pistols* was finally being released. John was expecting to sell a lot of copies because the big shops were refusing to stock it. On the Friday it came out, he put three of the lurid yellow and pink LP covers in the centre of the window display. It was not long before he had a visit from the police. They said there had been complaints - people were affronted by the word 'bollocks'. He was given the choice of taking them down or covering up the offending word. John, mindful that his grumpy dad still owned the shop - even if he had left its running to his son – wanted to avoid any trouble. He took the second option and covered up the 'bollocks' with stickers with 'censored' written on them.

As soon as I got there in the morning, John said not to bother breaking up cardboard boxes like I usually did at the start of the day; he wanted me serving in the shop as soon as it opened. I got the impression that he wanted to show his commitment to the LP that we had all been waiting for by having a punk behind the counter. Just before he unlocked the door, he told me to play the LP - loudly. I placed a copy on the turntable and put the needle on the record; the jackboots that introduced Holidays in the Sun crunched through the speakers and then gave way to the crashing chords of the guitar. It sounded superb. John propped the door open and everyone who passed the shop looked in; but later, when the song Bodies came on, there was so much swearing that he frantically signalled to me to stop it. I moved the needle on to the next song and we did this all morning as we continued to play nothing else.

There was a steady stream of customers in the first couple of hours, and we sold quite a few copies of the LP, but by late morning the shop was packed and everyone who came to the counter asked for the Sex Pistols; even when they had their copy, they stayed in the shop listening or chatting with their friends. By lunchtime, we had sold every copy we had. In the afternoon Colin Cummings came into the shop; he was on his own and hovered by the door for a while. I watched him flick through the racks of covers and then, eventually, he came up to the counter. Without acknowledging who he was, I politely asked if I could help him. He asked for the Sex Pistols LP. I pretended not to hear him. I turned the music down a little – we were playing Iggy Pop, now - and asked him to repeat it. When he did, I said, "I'm sorry, we've sold out. You're too late."

I had stayed up late on Saturday night listening to the "Heroes" LP, so I laid in bed on Sunday morning. Like *Low*, side two of Bowie's new LP was mostly instrumentals. It was as though the side ones together were one LP and the side twos another. I preferred the proper songs but I had increasingly played the electronic pieces because they were perfect late-night listening.

I finished reading my book: Arthur ended up planning to marry the young girl, Doreen. Despite all his supposed rebellious wildness, he was going to settle down. It made me think that Gary was right; that was what you were expected to do and you might as well do it sooner rather than later and avoid all the sound and fury.

Dad stuck his head in my room late in the morning. He said they were cooking a roast and they wanted Deborah to come over, so would I go to her flat and tell her. This was interesting. We had got into the habit of hardly ever having a proper Sunday dinner; Dad and Shirley went to the pub most Sunday lunchtimes and we usually ate the seafood they came back with in the late afternoon. The last time Deborah had been invited for Sunday dinner was when the announcement about Shirley moving in was made. On reflection, this was not interesting but worrying.

Gary opened the door to me at Deborah's. "Alright, Billy boy? What do you think of the Pistols LP, then? Blinding, ain't it?"

I agreed with him and said my favourite track was EMI, where they took the piss out of the record companies that had signed them and then dropped them. "So, this is your home, now, Gary?"

He broke into a broad grin. "Yeah. You'll have to get used to my ugly mug being around all the time."

Deborah also thought that a family Sunday dinner was worrying and said she would be there by one o'clock. "Do you think it would be alright if Gary came?"

I was flattered that she was asking my advice and I said I was sure Dad would be fine with it. I thought that whatever news Dad and Shirley Twinset were going to announce, having Gary there would mean we outnumbered them.

There was an uneasy atmosphere when we were all in our flat. I could tell Gary felt it because he busied himself with little Michael and avoided any conversation. Deborah kept asking Dad questions about his plans but he gave short non-committal answers and I sensed he was saving anything he had to say until we were all sitting down to eat. Shirley was in the kitchen cooking the chicken and every time Dad went in there, we could hear her snapping at him as though he was Johnnie to her Fanny Cradock.

The only alcohol on the table was Dad's home brewed beer and I noticed that, when Shirley sat down, she was drinking water. I wondered if they were cutting back now that they were going to be unemployed. The conversation was awkward and the redundancies at the factory were not mentioned. Dad talked about the football and moaned that there had only been two wins all season. Then Gary mentioned a story that had been in all the newspapers about a Mormon who had been kidnapped by a beauty queen and held prisoner as her sex slave. Dad asked what the bloke was complaining for but his joke fell flat when Shirley reminded him that me and little Michael were present. Deborah said the woman and the Mormon were both from America which seemed to explain it for everyone.

I helped Deborah clear away the dinner plates while Shirley served us up Arctic Roll for afters. When we were in the kitchen together, Deborah asked me what was going on. There was a reason for the family Sunday dinner but nothing had happened yet. She said the suspense was killing her.

Gary commented on how nice the Arctic Roll was; I was not sure if he was taking the mickey or not. Shirley said she had got it from Bejam and how cheap everything was in there. The small talk was reaching new levels of banality and I just wanted Dad to put us out of our misery and say something about the future.

When we had finished eating, he suddenly said he had some important things to say that affected us all. Clearly, what he was about to reveal had been rehearsed and Shirley had agreed he should take the lead. They both looked very grave.

"As you know, it's me and Shirley's last day at the factory tomorrow. And because we've both lost our jobs, we need to make some changes."

I knew it, Deborah was right; we were moving to bloody Bracknell.

"Firstly, and with deep regret, Shirley is moving out this week and going back to stay with her sister, June, in Bromley."

This was great news. Now there was no money coming in, the heartless gold-digger was dumping Dad and running off to find another fool.

"Shirley has not been happy here for a while. Having her ex-husband living downstairs was always going to be difficult and there have been tensions."

Tensions? You could say that. You punched him in the face and he threw Shirley's Elvis records off the landing.

"So, we were thinking of making changes anyway. But June works at a small electronics firm and there's an opening for Shirley now and there might be one for me soon. So it makes sense if she goes down to Bromley and I follow her as soon as I can."

They were not splitting up and he was going to move, as well. Why had I not been mentioned?

"There's not room for me and Billy at June's but I've advertised for a mutual exchange on the flat and applied to the Council for a transfer. As we've got a three-bedroomed flat, and we're only after two bedrooms, there's a good chance we'll get something in Bromley either way. Me and Billy will stay here until it comes through."

Bromley? I was moving to Bromley. I was speechless but Deborah spoke for me. "What about Billy's school?"

"Ah, yes. This is where you come in Deborah. Billy has seven or eight months left until he leaves school. There's a chance the flat will come through before then so, if it does, I thought he could stay with you until he finishes school and then come down to Bromley when he's done his exams."

Deborah opened her mouth. She had a look on her face that said, 'You've worked this all out, haven't you, Dad?' but she said nothing. Instead, she squeezed my arm and then eventually said, "Of course he can." She looked at Gary.

I could tell he was put out and I knew what he was thinking: just as I get something approaching my own family life started, this happens. But then he smiled, punched me on the shoulder and said, "Yeah, Billy boy's always welcome."

120

I was not sure whether to laugh with delight at the simple warmth of my sister and Gary or shout with anger at the cold callousness of my Dad and Shirley Twinset.

NOVEMBER

Shirley moved out on a Monday when I was at school. When I got home after rehearsing with the group, her flamenco dolls and Elvis records had all gone and the boxes of her stuff that she had never unpacked were no longer cluttering up the hallway and Deborah's old room. Dad looked forlorn sitting on the settee on his own. I could tell he was feeling sorry for himself but any sympathy I might have had for him was tempered by his unfeeling attitude towards me. The Sunday dinner announcement had been the first I had heard of his plans and, even after we had all been able to digest his news, he made no attempt to ask me how I felt. Living with Deborah and Gary would be good but I would have to move out once I had finished my exams in the summer. My only hope was if they let me live with them indefinitely; if they did, I would have to come up with a good reason why to convince Dad; total privacy for him and Shirley might be enough justification.

Rehearsals had been going well: my coordination and stamina had both improved and, although I still would not say I could play the drums properly, I could keep the rhythm going at a fast pace. Kev had been influenced by the sound of Siouxsie and the Banshees and was playing his guitar with lots of treble on it. He wanted the bass to be played at the same speed as his guitar but Dennis said there was no way he could; "I play syncopated bass," he kept saying, but neither of us knew what he meant. We sounded good, though; undoubtedly a punk group but slightly strange. And we had eight songs that we could play, two of them written by me and Kev. Most importantly, we had a name that we all thought was the best we had come up with: inspired by the big sex scandal in the newspapers, we were now called Mormon In Chains. Originally, I had suggested Mormon Sex In Chains, which was one of the headlines I had seen, but Kev said the youth club would not allow that on the poster advertising our performance.

There were some problems, though: Tina was practising in Kev's bedroom with only him on guitar, and the first time she would sing with us all together would be at the youth club; Dennis was still very unhappy about playing on stage in a punk rock group and he had said that, after the youth club, he would not do any more performances and we would have to find someone else to play bass; although Dennis was getting a guitar amp from his brother for Kev to use, I had no drums. This last problem was giving me sleepless nights. We had asked Mr Mitchell if we could borrow the school drum kit; he had said he would like to help but it was out of the question. Kev said we might have to do it without drums and I could play something else; but Mags was coming along to watch and I saw it as a chance to make a good impression on her. If I was on stage playing the tambourine, I would look ridiculous.

The following Saturday, I was walking home from work when I saw Mole's van parked up on the street ahead of me; it was dark and the streetlights were dim but it was definitely his van. My instinct was to try and get past without him noticing me but I could see a cloud of smoke and I knew his window was down; before I had time to act, his head popped out and he called to me, "Alright, man. What you up to?"

He looked scruffier than ever and his hair was in need of a wash. I was nervous because the last time I had seen him was when he stormed out of Deborah's flat. I told him about Mormon In Chains and my job at the record shop.

He pointed to the bag I was carrying. "What you bought? Don't tell me - punk rock? Elvis Costello?"

I took out the new Ramones LP I had bought and the single by Buzzcocks that John had given me for free. "Elvis Costello isn't really punk, Mole."

"That's weird," he said, looking at the cover of Orgasm Addict. "That bird's got an iron for a head and mouths for tits."

"It's a collage," I said in the most patronising voice I could muster. And then quickly added, "Are you going to see little Michael?"

His face dropped. "Well, I would if your mate wasn't living there. No, I've been doing a bit of overtime in there." He pointed at a

123

building behind me that was halfway through being refurbished. "I'm just waiting for the geezer to come and pay me."

I had an idea. "Will you be here next Saturday? The group I'm in are playing at the youth club and I could do with your help."

He smiled and I could see that his teeth were yellow. "I'll be working here next week but I can't help you, man. I'm not musical."

"It's more your van, I need - and you, of course. It'll take all evening but I could give you five pounds."

"Oh, I get you - you want me to be your roadie. That's cool, I can do that, man. What time?"

"I'll meet you here at the same time next Saturday. You won't let me down, will you, Mole?"

A man came out of the building and handed some money to him through the window. Mole counted the notes and then started up his van. "You can rely on me, man."

The next night we went down to Croydon again; Gary was not there to accompany us – he was playing happy families with my sister - a fact I forgot to mention to my dad, but there was quite a crowd of us on the bus. Some of the high street punks went, too, and Lorraine got on with a friend in Bromley. We were being quite noisy and attracted some attention: the conductor told us to quieten down or he would kick us off the bus and a drunk man said they should bring back National Service to sort us all out. As we were getting off the bus, an old lady said that we looked like some sort of weird third sex, which made us all shriek with laughter.

Buzzcocks were playing and the queue outside was longer than it had been on our previous two visits; but Lorraine saw a group of girls that she knew in the line and we pushed in with them. While we were waiting to go in, a car pulled up and Colin Cummings and Nick Phillips got out. Phillips' hair was shorter and they were both wearing straight-legged jeans. As the car pulled away, I saw that it was being driven by Caroline, Cummings' mum. They walked past us to join the back of the queue and Kev shouted out, "Poseurs!"

The support group were The Lurkers, who I had heard doing a session on John Peel. They sounded a lot like the Ramones - really fast – and they got the crowd fired up; the no-pogo-dancing

124

announcement was, again, spectacularly ignored. We went back into the bar area before Buzzcocks came on and Kev and Tina went and bought some beer because they looked the oldest. We were all in a raucous mood and I felt for the first time that I was truly part of something; I was one of a large and loud crowd of friends - and I belonged.

I saw Cummings and Phillips across the room; they were with a small group of plastics. They saw me staring at them and one of them must have said something to the others because they all turned around and looked in my direction. It was then that I realised one of them was Sophie. The big brown eyes, the impish face and the long dark hair; it was unmistakeably her and she still looked beautiful. But she was wearing a black bin liner, covered in safety pins and badges, as a jacket and she had a roll-neck jumper and flared jeans on underneath; she looked ridiculous - out of place and out of time. It seemed like a lifetime ago that I had first seen her and, now, I knew she belonged to the past. When she met my eyes, I turned away and started laughing at something Lorraine had said.

It was raining and cold when I left work on the following Saturday. I had come to hate rain as it could make my spiky hair flat in seconds but I hated the cold more because I never had enough clothes on to keep warm; a t-shirt and an Oxfam suit jacket were no protection against the November chill. All week I worried whether I could rely on Mole, given his track record. I was convinced he would not be there when I left work on the next Saturday but, when I reached the street I had seen him in a week before, there he was sitting in his van again, smoking. We had to wait until he got paid and then, when the man had been and gone, I asked Mole to drive around to the back of the school. We parked up and I gave him the five pounds I said I could pay him; I half thought that he might refuse it but he took it readily.

We had rehearsed in the music room on the previous evening and, when I had lugged the drums back to the store cupboard next to the tuck shop at the top of the playground, I had put the shackle of the padlock in place to make it look as though it was locked but had not pushed it down into the body. I just hoped that the caretaker had not noticed and locked it on his rounds.

"Right, we're picking up a drum kit," I said to Mole as I got out of the van. He followed me to the fence at the end of the playground where I lifted up a section that I knew was not secured.

"Here, this is a bit dodgy ain't it, man," said the dodgiest person that I knew.

"It's alright. I'm just borrowing it. We're bringing it back later on, after we've played." I felt sick to my stomach about what I was doing but I had no choice. The high street punk gang were going to be at the youth club and so were a lot of kids from school; and, above all, Mags was going to be there. I had made myself look stupid too many times and I was determined that it was not going to happen tonight.

Mole shrugged. "If you say so, man."

We went under the fence and walked across the playground. There were no lights on in the school or the caretaker's house. I was momentarily disorientated but eventually I found the cupboard. I had to use Mole's lighter to see the padlock; it was still unlocked. I felt relieved. It took us three trips to get the kit from the cupboard to Mole's van. The bass drum would not fit through the gap in the fence and Mole had to get some pliers from his van and snip through some more of the chain links to lift it up high enough.

We were all meeting at the youth club at six o'clock so I had no time to go home. Dennis and his brother were trying to get amps out from the back seat of a car when we pulled up outside. Me and Mole ferried the drum kit in and I started putting it together on the low stage. The youth worker was setting up two microphones and kept saying, "One, two. One, two." The DJ's turntables were next to the stage and he was sorting through his records. Kev and Tina arrived with Lorraine; Kev looked puzzled when he saw the drums and then he realised where they were from. He looked at me with a furrowed brow. "How come you've got these? Did Mitchell change his mind? Billy, have you got permission?"

"I've just borrowed them. Mole's helping me. We'll put them back before they're missed. Don't worry about it."

126

He exhaled and shook his head. "Fucking hell, Billy. I hope you know what you're doing." Dennis was behind him and I heard him suck his teeth.

Mole came up to the stage. "Look, no offence, man, but I don't really want to hang around all night. Punk's not my thing and I 've got to see a man about a dog. I'll come back later. What time?"

I told him that it would be over by ten o'clock and he should come back then. "You will come back, won't you Mole?"

"You can rely on me, man. See you later." He scurried off and I had a terrible feeling that he would leave me in the lurch and I would be left with the task of trying to smuggle a drum kit back into school on my own. I had not thought through how much I was depending on Mole; now it was all I could think about.

We had time to play one song to make sure we sounded right before the club opened. Dennis had got himself a chair and sat down to play his bass at the back of the stage next to me, which meant that Kev and Tina were the most visible members of the group. This was good because they looked fantastic: Kev was wearing a sinister black boiler suit his dad had got him from work; he had written GUTTERSNIPE on the breast pocket and across the back in silver, and he had painted the words BULLSHIT DETECTOR on his guitar. Tina was wearing Lorraine's leather jacket and had put loads of black make-up around her eyes. She was wearing high-heeled shoes and her hair was teased up really high; she looked so tall and intimidating. We did our second original song, Factory Job; with Tina singing, it sounded tremendous: angry and hopeful at the same time.

Kev had written out a list of the songs for each of us, in the order that we were playing them:
Blitzkrieg Bop
You Really Got Me
Career Opportunities
Lewisham
Factory Job
Newtown
Judy Is A Punk
Let's Dance

We had decided to start with Blitzkrieg Bop, to get everyone going, and to play our own songs right in the middle, because they were the most important to us; we would finish with Let's Dance, because it was the most upbeat one we played. I stuck my list on top of the bass drum with a piece of Sellotape where I could see it.

The youth club started to fill up. I had not considered what most of the audience would be like but it was obvious that most of them would not like punk. There were lots of hard kids who looked like they would not be easily impressed by Mormon In Chains; but the high street punks had arrived and there were a few spiky-haired boys from school. However, there was no sign of Mags. The more I had thought about it, the more I wondered why she would give up a Saturday night to come to a kids' youth club on our estate; she was probably not going to show up.

The records that were being played by the DJ were completely inappropriate: girls were dancing to Yes Sir I Can Boogie and Black Is Black and then some boys joined in when the DJ put Queen and Status Quo on; but as it got nearer the time for us to perform, he did compromise by playing Tom Robinson and Jonathan Richman.

The DJ signalled that it was time for us to go on stage. I was breathing really hard out of fright and excitement. I looked at Dennis; he was thoroughly fed up. I could tell that Tina and Kev were nervous; Tina gritted her teeth at me in mock fear. She went up to the microphone and said, "Good evening ladies and germs. We are Mormon In Chains and this is Blitzkrieg Bop." It was then that I noticed that Mags was right at the front of the stage because she whooped and started leaping around with another girl as the music began.

It was like running the 800 metres again: I was surprised by how fast we had set off and I thought I would never be able to keep up the pace; but I did. When she practised You Really Got Me, Tina had changed the word 'girl' to 'boy', but now she reverted back to 'girl', which made the song quite shocking. We messed up Career Opportunities but the large body of people jumping around in front of us did not seem to notice or care. I caught sight of Gary, standing at the back of them, smiling.

128

Our own songs did not go down as well as we thought they would – probably because no one knew them – and I was grateful for The Slits song because it slowed down the pace. When we launched into our second Ramones track, I saw that some of the hard boys had joined the throng, a little too enthusiastically, and a few kids got knocked over.

Tina announced our last song and shouted, "And everyone needs to get up and dance!" This was taken literally: as soon as I started drumming, people climbed on to the stage to dance along. Soon, all of the crowd who had been in front of the stage were on it. Twice, someone fell over into my drum kit and it moved back until I was so squashed up against the wall at the back of the stage that I could not play; the song petered out into a chaotic ending. From somewhere deep in the crowd in front of me, I could hear Tina intoning, "Let's dance," over and over again, even though the music had finished. The audience cheered and clapped as we got down from the stage. We had been good; I felt exhilarated.

Mags hugged me and introduced me to her friend, who had wild hair and looked as though she should be in The Slits. They both said we were great fun and they loved our version of You Really Got Me. Mags cuddled Tina and told her how amazing she had been. Lorraine kissed me on the cheek and said I had been brilliant and then spoiled it by shrieking, "Eugh! You're all sweaty!" Gary came over and said Deborah was expecting us all to go back to her flat. Over his shoulder, I saw Mole coming through the door with another scruffy bloke. I was relieved.

Gary turned around. "What's he doing here?"

"He's helping me with the drums, Gary. Don't cause any trouble."

"Alright, I won't. But don't be long. Debs wants to hear all about this evening." He ignored Mole as he walked past him.

When we went to pack away the gear, I saw that the skin on the front of the bass drum was ripped; someone must have put their foot through it. This was a disaster. Dennis looked down at it and said, "Those crazy kids. That's bad luck, Billy," which made me feel worse.

129

Kev tried to make me feel better. "That could have happened anytime. And school won't know you used them, anyway. Don't worry. Just get them back."

Mole's mate helped us with the drums and, with three of us, we quickly got them loaded into the van. Dennis had packed the amps into his brother's car and he came over and shook my hand. "It's been fun," he said without any sense of fun in his voice whatsoever. "Take it easy, Billy."

I felt sad that Dennis was leaving the group but glad he had helped us out and understood it was not his type of music. I asked him if he wanted to come to my sister's but he declined. "You take it easy, too, Dennis." I turned to Mole. "Shall we get these drums back, then?"

"Look, man. We can manage. You get off and enjoy yourself."

I was happy to accept his offer. I was exhausted and wanted to get to Deborah's to celebrate with the others. "Alright, cheers. Make sure you lock the padlock when you've put them back."

"Of course I will," he smiled, "you can rely on me, man."

I could hear the hum of music and the buzz of excited chatter as I waited outside Deborah's front door. When she eventually opened it, she said she wished she had been able to see me play but she had to stay with little Michael. "I hear you're like Animal from The Muppets - that's what Gary reckons," she added.

When I went into the front room, I was greeted with cries of, "Animal!" from Tina and Lorraine and the high street punks. They had obviously been talking about me, which I took as a compliment.

"That's what we should have called ourselves," I said. "The Electric Mayhem."

Kev threw a cushion at me. "No! We're sticking with Mormon In Chains. Everyone's been saying what a great name it is."

There were other people in the room that I had never seen before and they were all being quite loud; I wondered if Deborah was happy with so many teenagers in her flat. I went to the kitchen to look for her and found Mags and her friend. They had their arms around each other's waists; I realised they were more than just friends.

Mags ruffled my hair and said to her friend, "I gave this boy his first punk haircut in this very flat. I just hope he remembers the likes of us, down in the gutter, when he's up there with the stars."

"When was that?" I laughed.

"I don't know," she said. "Six months ago?"

Deborah appeared behind me. "No, it was longer ago than that. It was my flat-warming party in March."

It seemed a lifetime ago, I thought. I felt like a different person from the one who used to be scared just walking along the street. I asked Deborah if she was okay with all these kids in her flat. She shrugged her shoulders good-naturedly and said it was Gary who had brought them all back. "It's fine," she assured me.

I went and sat on the settee with Kev and we talked about who we could get to play the bass now Dennis had left. "One of this lot will just have to learn. It's not that hard. We've got to keep going now we've started. I enjoyed it so much tonight, Billy. I can't wait to do it again."

I stood on the balcony and watched the city lights dancing into the distance. Kev was right: we had to keep going; it was my only way of avoiding a factory job. I thought about what Mags had said to me when we went to see X-Ray Spex: "You can do whatever you want to do."

Lorraine came out and stood next to me. She rested her arms on the balcony rail and stared at the lights with me. "What are you thinking about?" she asked.

I could see her breath like smoke in the cold night air. "The future," I replied.

After the euphoria of the weekend, going back to school on Monday brought me down to earth with not so much a bump as a nagging worry. I was not sure the school drumkit was used that often and I wondered when the damage would be discovered, and if it would be traceable to me. We were not rehearsing at school until we had found another bass player, so I calculated that it might be days before anyone noticed the broken skin. I was wrong.

During first lesson in English, I saw Mr Mitchell walk past the classroom windows and stop at the door. Miss Kelly went out to him.

There was a brief conversation and she came back in and said, "Billy, Mr Mitchell would like to talk to you. Take your things with you." I flushed to the very roots of my hair as I got to my feet. I felt shaky.

Mitchell was not as friendly as he usually was and asked me to follow him. We walked down the corridor to the staircase at the far end – the one us boys were not allowed to use – and I knew that we must be going to see the Headteacher. We reached Old Burkett's office and he asked me to wait outside as he knocked quickly on the door and slipped inside. I felt dizzy.

I tried to think what I would say when they asked me about the damage. Kev said the school had no idea I had used the drums; he was right - I should simply say I knew nothing about it. But not only had I asked to borrow them at the weekend, I had been the last to use them on Friday. The next time Mitchell sees them, they have been damaged. I felt sick.

Before I could think any further, I had been whisked into the office. Like the last time I had been there, Old Burkett was behind his desk wreathed in cigarette smoke. When I had been there with McNally, I was asked to sit down; this time, I was made to stand. I felt faint.

Old Burkett balanced his cigarette on the edge of the ashtray and calmly looked up at me. "Now, Monson, I want you to tell me - truthfully and exactly - what you know about these drums."

I was about to lie and deny all knowledge, but at the last my courage failed me. "I'm sorry, sir. I'll pay for the damage," I blurted out. I turned to Mitchell. "I didn't mean to split the skin, sir. It was an accident."

They exchanged confused looks and then Old Burkett seemed to get angry. "Damage, Monson? Damage? They're not damaged, boy, they're not there!"

I felt the blood draining from my head to my toes and I must have passed out because the next thing I knew I was lying on Old Burkett's Persian rug, his secretary kneeling over me with a glass of water. They helped me into a chair, all three of them staring at me intently.

When they were satisfied that I was not going to collapse again, Old Burkett said, "Well, what have you got to say, Monson?"

There was only one word on my mind and only one word I could say. "Mole."

When the caretaker was opening up in the morning, he had noticed that the padlock on the store cupboard was open; he had gone to the Music department to ask if they could check if anything was missing. When Mitchell saw that the drumkit was not there, he had gone straight to the Headmaster.

I told them – truthfully and exactly – everything. How neither Kev nor Dennis knew what I was doing, how I had left the cupboard open, got under the fence, taken the drums with Mole and how I had entrusted him and his mate to take them back. I think Mitchell believed that I was intending to return them but I was not sure Old Burkett did. He told me that the police would need to be involved and that I was to be suspended, forthwith. I was to go straight home and he would ring my dad and tell him what had happened. I was to expect to be contacted by the police to make a formal statement.

I could hear the kids in the playground – at my school and the primary school next door – on their break as I went home. It struck me that there is no greater reminder of exclusion than hearing enjoyment at a distance. I walked slowly, to give Old Burkett plenty of time to telephone Dad so I would not have to explain. I was expecting him to be furious but, when I walked through the door, he came out into the hall to meet me and he looked as though he had been crying.

DECEMBER

Dad laid the blame for what had happened at many doors: me, for being stupid enough to rely on a toe rag like Mole; my sister, for her recurring returns home making for an unstable environment; school, for not being tough enough with the boys in its care and creating an atmosphere of ill-discipline; the estate we lived on, for having too many hard kids who were a bad influence; punk rock, for its complete disregard of authority; himself, as a single-parent, for failing me at a crucial time in my life. I was pleased – in a strange way – that he had included himself in this list; but I noticed that he was very careful not to include Shirley in his parade of the guilty and the effect her six-month sojourn in our flat might have had.

Dad had taken me to the police station the day after I was suspended and I had made a statement to a plain clothes policeman. I had to describe what I had done, when I had done it and who had been involved. He wrote out what I said - almost in my words - and then read back each sentence and asked me to agree if it was a fair representation before carrying on. I had to provide as much information as I could about Mole, and what I knew about where he lived and worked. Dad was in the room with me and he urged me to tell all. "Don't hold back, Billy. Tell them everything you know about that dirty bastard. You owe him nothing." The policeman had asked Dad if he would just let me tell the story. When we had finished, the full statement was read to me and I had to sign at the bottom to say it was a correct record of my version of events.

Deborah had been waiting at our flat when we came home from the police station. Kev had told Gary that I had been sent home from school and they knew it was connected to Mole and the drumkit. How they had known this, she had not been able say. She was angry at Mole; she thought he had taken the drums to get back at her and Gary and she alternated between saying, "How could he do this to my brother?" and, "I'll fucking kill him!" But mostly she was upset for me and in a sob-filled speech she had blamed herself. "I should have been a mum to you but I was too busy mothering Michael and

Mole. Michael needs me but I should have got rid of Mole years ago. What an idiot I've been to keep him wrapped around us – look where it's led."

It had upset me to see her so distressed and I told her not to blame herself. "The police will find Mole and then everything will be sorted out," I had told her, "and then we can have nothing to do with him ever again."

Just over a week passed and, in that time, the school had telephoned once to say that the police were still investigating the case and I would stay suspended until further notice. Gary, of course, had not wanted to leave things to the police: he had been touring Mole's known haunts with the intention of doing him harm if he found him; but there had been no sign of him.

Then, just as the temperature had dropped and the first of the winter sleet had started to fall, Dad was asked to go to the school on his own. I was glad I did not have to go with him; I had no wish to see the inside of Old Burkett's office again – I just wanted to go back to school. Miss Kelly was the only teacher who had given me some work to do while I was suspended: revising Romeo and Juliet in preparation for the mock exams after Christmas. Kev had brought the work to the flat and commiserated with me over Mole's treachery; but he had also made it clear that he thought I was stupid for trusting him, something I had heard enough from my dad. Kev was one of the few people I had seen outside of my family. Even though I had been to work, I asked John if I could be excused from serving in the shop as I felt ill; the truth was, I wanted to avoid seeing any of the high street punks.

On his return from the school, Dad sat down wearily in the kitchen without taking his coat off and asked me to make a cup of tea. I was perhaps imagining it but, since he had been made redundant and I had been suspended, he was looking older; and now, his demeanour told me there was bad news. But after a long gulp of tea, he said the opposite. "There's good news, Billy. The police have arrested Mole."

I felt an enormous sense of relief. "How did they catch him?"

135

"There was a warrant out and he was stopped in his van for a traffic offence. He admitted that he'd nicked the drums and sold them to a second-hand music shop in New Cross. They've been recovered and the school have got them back. He's been charged with theft and he goes to court next week."

The mention of arrest and court had made what happened suddenly seem criminal. "What about me?"

"Well, there's more good news: you're not going to be charged. But you will get a juvenile police caution. It means you won't be convicted but there will be a note of it on your record."

My record. That sounded bad. "That doesn't sound like good news, Dad," I said.

"Well, it is, son. You were very close to being charged with theft. But you're not and that's part of the good news. Because there's also some bad news."

I knew it. I could tell as soon as he got home that it had not gone well.

"They don't want you back at school, Billy. You've been expelled."

Expelled. What an idiot I had been. Of course I was being expelled; I had stolen school property. I had become convinced that everything could return to normal; but I had been deluding myself. I was a fool. I thought of Romeo and what he said when he had messed everything up: I was fortune's fool.

The only thing I could think to do was to retreat to my room and seek solace in my David Bowie records. I played the *Space Oddity* LP several times; a lot of the lyrics were sad or dark and, even though I did not understand all of them, they chimed with how I was feeling. At the end of side two, I kept lifting the needle back to play the penultimate track, God Knows I'm Good, about an old lady who, uncharacteristically, steals a tin of stewing steak from a supermarket. She faints when she is caught. I had no belief in God but I was sure I was good; I had been stupid, but I was not bad. Expulsion was for hard kids. Like when Danny Holland smashed a chair over John Pisani's head in assembly. That was the company I was keeping, now.

Dad knocked on my door and asked if I wanted beans on toast. We ate in the kitchen in silence; he had no idea how to make the situation any better and I had nothing to say. I went back to my room and sat by the window. The sleet was driving across the estate, horizontally; a road sweeper, buried deep inside his council donkey jacket. was pushing his cart through the courtyard. That looked like an even worse job than working in a factory. I wondered how many O Levels he had; he probably had none, maybe some CSEs. I was unlikely to get any qualifications at all, now. It would be my birthday in a couple of months; the hard kids said you could leave school at Easter if you were sixteen. Perhaps I could just stay at home until then and become a road sweeper.

In the afternoon, Dad said he was going over to Deborah's. I watched him walking off through the estate until he disappeared from view. Soon after, as the light was fading, kids coming home from school started to appear. I saw Tina coming towards the block; she was holding one hand above her head, trying to stop her hair from going flat in the sleet. She had been incredible at the youth club; what it must have taken to stand at the front of the stage and display such confidence. I could only ever have been up there hiding behind the drums; now, I never wanted to see a drum kit again. I thought about Lorraine: she had kissed me on the cheek at the youth club and, on Deborah's balcony, stood very close to me. I felt we had wanted to say something more to each other, but neither of us did.

It was fully dark when Dad got home. He came to check if I was alright and then, soon after, I heard him in the hallway on the telephone. He was talking to Shirley; I could hear him telling her about his meeting at the school. He used the word 'nightmare' more than once. When he said the phrase 'dirty bastard' I knew he had moved on to Mole. He repeated what Deborah had said, several times: "I'll fucking kill him." They moved on to discussing jobs: how hers was going and his chances of getting work at the electronics firm. Dad mentioned something about the council and the housing transfer but he was speaking in a much quieter voice and I could not hear what he said.

On Friday evening, Kev and Tina called round. They had heard I had been expelled and wanted to know where I was going to go to school; I said I had no idea. It was not something me and Dad had discussed but I was going to have to talk to him about it soon. They asked if I fancied going to the youth club with them but, before I could answer, Kev said he would understand if I would rather not. I sensed that they were asking because they felt they should and were relieved when I declined. Even if I had wanted to go, I would not have dared ask Dad.

I went to work in the morning. I had not told John anything about what had happened at school and I hoped he did not know; he might sack me if he found out I had been involved in stealing. I had to do some serving in the shop but, thankfully, no one I knew came in. It was all Christmas shoppers buying greatest hits LPs by singers like Cliff Richard and Gladys Knight. At lunchtime, Deborah and Gary were waiting outside the shop for me with little Michael. They took me to the restaurant in the big department store and we had fish, chips and peas. The conversation was stilted and even Gary struggled to make small talk. When he took little Michael off to the toilet, Deborah started talking about me being expelled. "How are you feeling?" she asked.

I simply shrugged because I was not sure how to explain how I felt; I knew it was Mole's fault as much as, if not more than, my own but I was beginning to develop a sense of shame over what I had done.

"And what do you think about going to school in Bromley?"

This stunned me. "Bromley? What do you mean?"

Deborah realised I knew nothing about this. "Hasn't Dad talked to you? He thinks you should start at a school down that way because you'll be moving there soon, anyway."

I had really mucked things up. Before, I had consoled myself about the housing transfer with the thought that, if it came through soon, I would go and live with my sister until I left school. And then…well, I had not thought that far ahead but I imagined that I could find a way of never going to live with my dad and Shirley in Bromley. Now, things were falling apart.

Gary and little Michael sat back down again. "Everything alright?"

No, it was not. Everything was as far away from alright as it was possible to be.

After work, I got home as quickly as I could. Dad apologised for not having spoken to me first, but he said he wanted to be certain before he outlined any plans. He had already been offered a flat in Bromley and now he had spoken to the council there about me starting in one of their schools after Christmas. "We can go down and look at the flat next week and we might be able to tie it in with a visit to one of the schools, if you like."

I nodded mutely and thought of the Sunday dinner a couple of months before and how matter-of-factly he had laid out what was going to happen as a result of the redundancies; my expulsion meant his plans just required a small adjustment. If he had been upset about the drums incident at first, he was not showing it now; he was busy organising the future - my future.

On the bus to Bromley with Dad, it felt so different from when I had last been on that route, heading to Croydon with Kev and Tina and the rest of the high street punk tribe. For a start, we were sitting downstairs and my dad was having a running conversation with the bus conductor about the shortcomings of where we had just come from and the virtues of where we were heading to, which I sensed was for my benefit. Secondly, my hair was the flattest it had been for nine months - at Dad's absolute insistence - and I was wearing my school uniform, although without the tie and the badge, which Dad had cut off of my blazer breast pocket.

We got off the bus after we had reached the centre of Bromley and walked down several streets of identical houses. Dad had a hand-drawn map which he rotated each time we turned into a different road. Eventually, we stopped at a house which had two front doors side by side and a man from the council was standing in the front garden. He shook Dad's hand and we went through the righthand door, which opened straight on to a narrow set of stairs that went up; I realised it was not a house but two flats.

139

The flat seemed large, even though it only had two bedrooms; but there was no furniture in it at all, which probably made it appear bigger. I looked out of the front room window: the street was quiet and oppressive and its uniformity gave me a tightness across my chest. I could hear Dad wittering on somewhere else in the flat. I would have given anything to turn back the clock to a time before I was kicked out of school and he was kicked out of work - to a time before Mum died.

We left the flat and began to retrace our steps to the main road. The visit had clearly put Dad in a good mood. "What did you think? It's a good flat, isn't it?" He was not expecting me to answer. "And in a nice street, as well." We walked along the main road for a while and then we went up a long, wide tree-lined road that had no houses on it. At the top, set well back, was a school in the middle of its own playing fields. These kids had no need to go to the rec for their sports day, I thought. The building was more modern than my school and there was much more outdoor space – even the playgrounds were large. We went down the driveway and in through tall glass doors.

Inside the entrance, it was hushed and polished. The secretary asked us to wait, in what she called the vestibule. We sat on some plump leather armchairs. The walls were lined with paintings and framed group photographs of boys who had left the school years before. The secretary came out again and said, "Mr Monson, will you follow me, please?" When she saw me getting up as well, she made it clear that I was to stay where I was. Dad followed her across the lobby and they went through the door marked HEADMASTER. While I waited, a bell rang and I heard the increasing clamour of boys' footsteps and voices. A few of them passed through the entrance hall and looked my way without expression. Dad was gone a long time and when he finally came out we left the building straight away. I was relieved that I did not have to go to the Headmaster's office but puzzled that we did not look around the school. I said as much to Dad and it seemed to annoy him.

"Look, Billy. You've been expelled. This is the only place round here that said they'll have you. They're not going to take us on a jolly little tour of the school to try and impress us. They don't need you – but you need them. And you're going to have to watch your step. That Headmaster's a tough character. You need to get your head down and do some hard work or he'll be after you. You need some qualifications."

We walked back into the centre of town and went for a cup of tea in a café. I ate an iced bun while Dad read the newspaper. He started moaning about the England football team failing to qualify for the World Cup again and saying that Brian Clough should be made manager. The World Cup was in the summer; it would be starting just as the exams were finishing. That was all I had to do – make it through the next six months. I asked Dad when I was starting at the school.

"It was meant to be January but they want you to start before the Christmas holidays. You're going in for the last three days of term to ease yourself in. But it's also so they can see what you're like. You'd better keep your nose clean, Billy."

Yes, I thought, I suppose I can manage not to walk off with another drumkit. "When are we moving into the new flat?"

"Well, that won't be until January. You'll have to get the bus until we move. Or you could stay at Shirley's sister's."

It might be a long bus journey but I would rather do that than be cooped up with Shirley Twinset. Although, Lorraine would be there, which would be good; but I wondered what she thought of me now.

"Come on, finish your tea. We're going round there now."

It was dark outside and it had started to snow; the shop fronts lit up the wet pavement. We passed a record shop that had a display of punk singles in the window; there were some kids in school uniform hanging around inside. I would have to travel to work by bus in the future, unless I could get a job in there; that was unlikely, though.

Shirley opened the door with a cry of, "Ronnie!" She kissed my dad and then said, "And how's our little troublemaker?" to me. Shirley's sister made us a cup of tea and we sat in the front room drinking it. There was no sign of Lorraine. I felt awkward.

They talked about me staying there on school nights until we moved flat but I could tell Shirley's sister was not keen. "You'd have to sleep on the settee," she said, "and it's not very comfy."

"Unless he wants to share with your Lorraine," Shirley laughed and they all shrieked; I went bright red in the face. "Where is she, anyway?"

"Doing her homework, I think. Or listening to that bloody punk rock," her mum said. "I'll go and fetch her."

Lorraine came in and sat down. She smiled at me but there was an unusual awkwardness about her, too. The grown-ups carried on talking; Dad telling Shirley about the flat and she telling him that he was going to have an interview after Christmas at the electronics firm. "You'll get it easily, Ronnie. They need reliable people like you."

I had drunk too much tea so I asked where the toilet was and went upstairs. When I came back down, Lorraine was in the hallway. "I just wanted to say how sorry I am about what happened, Billy. That Mole's a bastard to do that to you." She kissed me on the cheek. "We'll see each other soon, yeah?" I nodded.

The front room door opened and Shirley came out with the tea cups. "Ooh, you two talking about that horrible music?" she said, on her way to the kitchen.

We both smiled and Lorraine called after her, "Yes, Aunty Shirley, that's right." I squeezed her hand and we went back in and sat down.

I went back down to Lorraine's the evening before my first day at the new school. I was dreading the morning: my new teachers would all know that I had been expelled and would think I was a thief. The other boys would perhaps not know I had been expelled; I could say that I had just moved to the area, which would almost be the truth. There was no opportunity to spend any time with Lorraine; we all sat and watched *Porridge*, which was funny, and then a *Play for Today*, which none of us could understand. Lorraine's mum turned off the telly before it finished and they all went up to bed. I took the cushions off the settee and laid them on the floor and slept on top of them in a sleeping bag.

We all left at the same time in the morning. I was hoping to be able to talk to Lorraine but her school was in the opposite direction to mine, so we parted at the front gate. I walked through the town centre with the commuters all hurrying down to the train station, bent against the icy winter rain. On the other side of town, I began to see boys up ahead wearing the same uniform as my new one. A few of them turned and looked at me, a stranger in their daily routine.

I had to report to the secretary when I arrived at school and I was made to wait in the same chairs that I had sat in with Dad. Even though he was not a great comfort, I wished Dad was with me now. A tall man in a grey suit, that perfectly matched the colour of his hair, stood in front of me, looking down. "Monson? Would you like to come with me?" He led me across to the same door Dad had gone through. I assumed the tall man was the Headmaster but, when the door swung back, there was already a man sitting behind the desk. He was bald and wore little round glasses; he reminded me of Captain Mainwaring in *Dad's Army*.

"Sit down." He beckoned to a chair. "Now, Monson. I want you to know that we are giving you a second chance – a second chance you are very lucky to have, given what you got up to at your previous school. And I want you to know that the boys who come to this school are no different to the boys at your last school; we have all types and shapes and sizes here. The difference is, we have discipline, strong discipline. The boys know what we expect of them and they know, if they fall below standard, they will be punished. In your case, any need for punishment will mean that your time with us will be very short, indeed. Do I make myself clear?"

I was not expecting a particularly warm welcome, but this seemed as cold as the weather outside. "Yes, sir," I mumbled.

"Good. Now, here is your timetable. The Deputy Head will take you to your form room. I will be collecting reports on your behaviour from your teachers and I will see you here after school at the end of the day."

I followed the Deputy Head down the wide corridor and we went out of a door and crossed a playground. We entered another building and went upstairs; there was a series of art rooms and we went to the one at the very end. I was ushered in and introduced to my new form tutor. I was told to sit at the table at the back with three other boys. The teacher was reading out details of a skiing trip. Everyone was listening intently. Then, the boy next to me kicked my foot to attract my attention and said, "So, what did you get expelled for?" I looked the other way.

Another boy, who was in the same lessons as me, was given the task of making sure I got to the classrooms. He was not interested in me and raced ahead; I had to make sure I kept sight of him otherwise I would have got lost. I was given new exercise books and I did all the work that the teachers set and kept my head down, like Dad had said I should do. I spoke to no one.

At break, a teacher collected me and spoke to me about my O Levels and CSEs. She explained that the school used a different exam board for some subjects and, in those lessons, I would have to go to the library and prepare for the summer exams on my own. That did not bother me but I was grateful that the discussion had spared me the ordeal of spending break time on my own. I still had lunch to get through, however.

I followed my escort to the canteen and queued up for school dinners. I sat at a table on my own that gradually filled with younger boys. They ignored me and carried on a fevered conversation around me about the *Star Wars* film that was being released during the Christmas break. I was putting my dirty plates on the trolley when I noticed a boy I recognised, queuing for food; he had a Neanderthal face above a broad chest, big arms and hands with banana fingers. It was Bunches: the kid who had chased me at the youth club in Bromley; the kid whose dad sold the *National Front News* at football; the kid whose dad had threatened me at the demonstration against the NF march. I was about to look away when he stared straight at me; it took him a moment, but I saw his brow furrow in thought and then his eyes narrow in recognition. I turned and walked quickly away.

When the final bell of the day sounded, I was coming down a staircase from the top of the school; through the glass, I could see kids streaming up the driveway and out of the school. Near the gate was a knot of motionless boys. Even at a distance, I could see that the one at the front, surveying the crowd, was Bunches; there was no doubt he was looking for me. I went to the Headmaster's office but I had to wait outside for some time. When he saw me, he told me that I had made a good impression on my teachers. "Hardworking and courteous, they say, Monson. It's a good start but you must keep it up." I was apprehensive leaving school but, to my relief, Bunches was no longer by the gate. He had missed me this time but I would not be able to avoid him forever.

When I got back to Lorraine's, I told her that I had seen Bunches and that he had been waiting for me outside school.

"Oh, yeah. I forgot about Darren. He's an idiot. He fancied me once but I told him to get lost. He doesn't like me anymore, now I'm into punk."

The last thing I wanted to do was admit to Lorraine that I was scared, so I put on a brave face. "I'll just tell him to get lost, too, then."

After we had tea, me and Lorraine played some records in the front room. She had the Sex Pistols LP and I had brought a couple of Ramones and Bowie records with me. Lorraine's mum saw the cover of *Aladdin Sane* and said, "Oh, do you like David Bowie? He used to go to your school, you know."

I wanted to avoid appearing rude but I had read a book about him and knew that he had gone to a different school. "No, I think he went to Bromley Technical High," I ventured.

"Yes, that's right. That's what your new school used to be called."

The next day, I walked to school as quickly as I could. When I got inside the building, I raced down the corridor to where the Headmaster's office was. I had worked out that he would have left school in 1963 and I scoured the group photographs for the right year. When I found it, I scanned the ranks of faces. He might have looked so different that he would be difficult to find; but then, there he was, in the second row from the back, standing in three-quarter profile, his face a portrait of nervousness and arrogance beneath a blonde quiff, the same age as me now, David Bowie. I put the side of my face against the cool glass and kept it there. I heard a laugh behind me but I did not turn around. I knew that everything was going to be alright.

#0061 - 101018 - C0 - 210/148/8 - PB - DID2325622